A TALE OF TWO PIPERS

An original novel by Emma Harrison

Based on the hit TV series created by

Constance M. Burge

Simon & Schuster, London

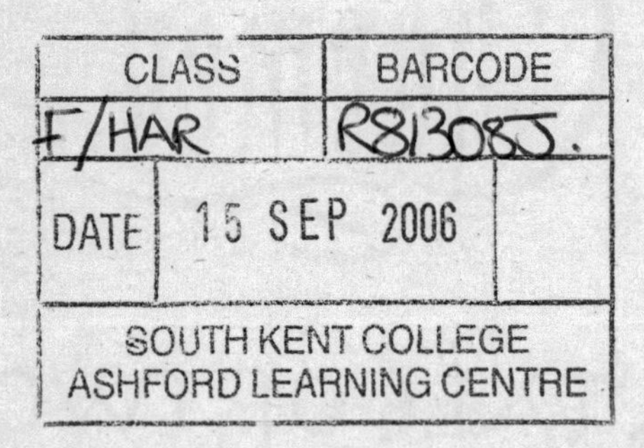

First published in Great Britain in 2004 by Simon & Schuster UK Ltd.
Africa House, 64–78 Kingsway, London WC2B 6AH
A Viacom Company

Originally published in 2004 by Simon Pulse,
an imprint of Simon & Schuster Children's Division, New York

A CIP catalogue record for this book is available from the British Library upon request.

ISBN 0689872720

3 5 7 9 10 8 6 4 2

Printed by Cox & Wyman Ltd, Reading, Berkshire

"I'LL GO TO THE INTERVIEW AND CHARM THE PANTS OFF THE REPORTER FROM THE CHRONICLE," PIPER TWO OFFERED.

"And I'll stay here and deal with the painters and any Darklighters that might show up," Piper One put in, smiling. "Then you can go to P3 and take care of Rinaldo while I bake!"

"Perfect!" Piper Two exclaimed.

They both stood up and started for the door that led to the foyer, but Piper One suddenly paused and grabbed Piper Two's arm. She immediately pulled her hand back. It was a little bizarre touching a person who was essentially herself. Now she knew what her body looked and felt like from the *outside* as well as the inside. This was way more intense than a mirror image. If she dwelled on it for too long, she knew it would freak her out.

"Wait a second," she said. "What about personal gain?"

"Hey. This is going to make us a much happier, saner witch," Piper Two told her, swinging her hair behind her shoulder. "It's for the greater good."

More titles in the

THE POWER OF THREE
KISS OF DARKNESS
THE CRIMSON SPELL
WHISPERS FROM THE PAST
VOODOO MOON
HAUNTED BY DESIRE
THE GYPSY ENCHANTMENT
THE LEGACY OF MERLIN
SOUL OF THE BRIDE
BEWARE WHAT YOU WISH
CHARMED AGAIN
SPIRIT OF THE WOLF
DATE WITH DEATH
GARDEN OF EVIL
DARK VENGEANCE
SHADOW OF THE SPHINX
SOMETHING WICCAN THIS WAY COMES
MIST AND STONE
MIRROR IMAGE
BETWEEN WORLDS
TRUTH AND CONSEQUENCES
LUCK BE A LADY
INHERIT THE WITCH

Chapter 1

Sunlight streamed through the kitchen windows of Halliwell Manor, warming Piper Halliwell's face and tickling her skin. But for the moment this witch was immune to the sun's natural cheering powers. Surrounded by contracts, bills, and to-do lists, a mug of coffee rapidly cooling in front of her, Piper was far too stressed to think about something as mundane as sunlight. She pushed up the long sleeves on her black T-shirt, pulled her chair closer to the table, and tried to decide on a game plan—an order in which to deal with the many things she had to deal with. Even prioritizing was tough.

Okay, I can make the phone calls I need to make now, then go to the supermarket, then P3 . . . but then I'll be late for that lunch meeting . . .

Wait, wait, wait. What if I go to P3 now, then *lunch,* then *make the phone calls . . .*

But then when am I going to bake?

Argh!

When Piper's younger sister Phoebe traipsed into the kitchen humming under her breath, Piper dropped her hands to the table and looked up.

"Good morning?" Phoebe said tentatively, noticing her sister's mood.

"Am I totally insane?" Piper asked.

Phoebe placed a large, open cardboard box on the island in the center of the room and looked her sister over, hands on her slim hips, as if she were seriously considering the question.

"Yes, you are. As evidenced by the fact that it is 10 A.M. on a Sunday and you are doing work," she said wryly. "What's the problem?"

"Me! I'm the problem!" Piper said, grasping an estimate for renovations to her nightclub, P3, in one hand and holding her forehead with the other. Her long brown hair spilled down over one shoulder, grazing the myriad papers on the table. She couldn't believe it was already ten. She'd been sitting here for an hour wasting time trying to figure out how to best use her time. "I have ten million things going on and no time to do any of them."

"So what else is new?" Phoebe said with a smile, crossing over to the coffeepot and pouring herself a full mug. She came around the island and leaned back against it, sipping at her java. Piper took in her sister's flowing pink skirt, her white halter top, and the haphazard curls that surrounded her face. The girl looked relaxed, happy, carefree. And Piper totally envied her. At the moment she couldn't remotely remember what it felt like to be that chill.

"You're right. Why do I always do this to myself?" she said to Phoebe, tossing the estimate across the table like a Frisbee. It hit a stack of papers and they tumbled to the floor. Great. Now she was going to have to reorganize *that* pile.

"Why do you always do *what* to yourself?" Paige Matthews, their half-sister and the youngest of the household, asked as she practically skipped into the room.

"Overextend," Piper said, getting up and turning her back on her table of work. The simple act of not looking at it made her feel ten times better already. Maybe if she ignored it, it would all just go away. She wished.

"Oh. Because you're Piper," Paige said with a shrug, shaking her hair back off her shoulders. "It's what you do."

Great, Piper thought. *Very comforting.* If overextending was in her nature, did that mean she was in for a lifetime of Sunday mornings like this one?

Paige pulled Phoebe's cardboard box closer to her and inspected the contents. Scrunching her nose, she picked up one of the tiny mesh sachets between two fingers and sniffed it. Her face registered pleasant surprise.

"Nice," she said with a smile. "Jasmine?"

"Among other things," Phoebe said, preening. "I was up all night tying the satin ribbons on them."

"Are they for the Star Kids event?" Paige asked.

"Yep!" Phoebe replied. "My work is officially done."

"Well, I thank you and the Star Kids thank you," Paige said, bowing her head slightly. "These are going to win me so many points with Joshua."

One of her friends at work, a guy named Joshua who just happened to be drop-dead gorgeous, had roped Paige into helping organize this year's charity fair for Star Kids—an organization that helped underprivileged children buy school supplies and computers and other things they would need to succeed. Always one to pay it forward, Paige had then roped her sisters into helping *her* help Joshua help the Star Kids.

"What are they?" Piper asked, joining Paige and pawing through the little pillows.

"They're wish charms," Phoebe said, leaning her elbows on the counter and sipping her coffee. "I left out a few ingredients so they won't pack too much of a punch, but they might bring a little luck to the kids."

"Good thinking," Paige said, dropping the charm in among the others. "I'm not sure the little ones could handle the power of a real Charmed Ones charm."

As the three most powerful witches of all

time, Piper, Phoebe and Paige had to watch themselves, even when doing something as innocent as whipping up party favors. Put a little too much Charmed Ones magic into something like a wish charm and it could cause major mayhem. Back in the early days, when the sisters had first gotten their powers, they were far more likely to slip up and risk exposing themselves and possibly even harming innocents instead of helping them. But by now they had learned what not to do.

For the most part, anyway.

"I can't believe you're already done with those," Piper said, shaking her head and feeling the sense of pressure bearing down on her again. "I haven't even finished my shopping yet."

"Piper! Let's get on the ball here!" Paige said lightly. "You're gonna make me look bad."

"Yeah, yeah, yeah," Piper said, snatching her shopping list from the table and looking it over.

She had agreed to bake a few dozen muffins and cupcakes for the charity fair. She had planned to get a start early in the week, knowing that she was going to have a lot of other things going on. It was only Sunday, but she already felt all of those things were piling up.

First off, P3 was going to be the venue for a huge fashion show the following weekend, showcasing the spring line of the famous international designer Rinaldo. The event was going to bring in a lot of business, but it had also become a major headache for Piper. It turned out that the designer and his entourage were very specific in their demands, on everything from lighting schemes to bouncers to bottled-water selection. Not only that, but Piper was up for the *San Francisco Chronicle*'s Businesswoman of the Year Award, for which she was supposed to be interviewed this week. To top it all off, she had a club to run, a family to feed, a husband to pay attention to, and most likely a few demons to vanquish.

A Charmed One's work was never done.

"Okay, well, we're off to the mall!" Paige said merrily, grabbing her bag.

Scratch that. *Some* Charmed Ones' work was never done.

"You guys are going to the *mall*?" Piper demanded.

"Yeah. I've got to get a new suit for the meeting with the advertising people on Wednesday," Phoebe told her, slinging her straw bag over her shoulder. Ever since Phoebe's advice column had taken off, the publicity people at her newspaper had been trying to find ways to maximize her exposure. This week they were presenting their ideas to Phoebe and her editor-in-chief, Elise.

"And I have a million errands to run," Paige put in.

"But I was hoping you guys would help me with some of this stuff," Piper said, her stress level mounting even further. What ever happened to sisterly support?

"Why don't you come with us?" Phoebe suggested, dumping the rest of her coffee in the sink. "Take a little break, get your mind off things?"

"Retail therapy is a proven method of stress reduction," Paige added with a nod, pursing her glossed lips slightly.

"I can't just blow all this off," Piper said, even though she was practically salivating to take them up on the offer. Looking around at the piles of paperwork just made her feel helpless, and she could hardly remember the last time she'd taken some time off to hang out with her sisters.

"Come on. You know you want to," Phoebe cajoled, knocking Piper with her hip.

Before Piper could answer, her husband, Leo, walked into the room, cupped her face in his hands, and planted a nice long kiss right on her lips. "Good morning," he said.

"Good morning," Piper replied, smiling. Leo was wearing jeans, a white T-shirt, and a brown-and-white flannel shirt. He looked ready for a long, lingering breakfast. But little did he know, that was not going to happen—not if Piper had anything to say about it.

"Good!" she said, clapping her hands on his shoulders. "Maybe *you* can help me."

Leo grimaced in that way he did whenever

he was about to let Piper down easy.

"What?" Piper asked. "What is it?"

"Well, actually, I have something I need to tell you guys. It's nothing bad!" he added quickly, reacting to their worried expressions. "It's just that there's a major shift of power taking place Up There, and I'm going to have a lot of meetings to attend," Leo told them. "I might not be able to orb right down if you call."

Piper sighed and dropped her hands to her sides. When she'd married a Whitelighter, she'd known what she was getting into. As a guardian angel to several witches, Leo had responsibilities to his other charges and to the Elders, the Powers That Be that sort of ran the supernatural show from above. The good side of the supernatural show, anyway. But that didn't change the fact that she sometimes felt deserted when he suddenly had to orb out to help someone else, or report to the Elders for something like this.

Especially when she was already at the end of her rope.

"And this is all happening now?" Piper asked.

"Soon. They're going to call all of us when they're ready to start," Leo told them.

"Wait a second, if you can't orb down when we call, what do we do if someone gets hurt?" Phoebe asked, her brow wrinkling.

"I'll be able to sense that and I'm sure they'll let me come if it's that urgent," Leo told them.

"Okay, well, if they're going to call you when

they're ready for you, then you might have time to help me first, right?" Piper said hopefully. "If you could just go to the supermarket, then I can—"

But when she turned around again, Leo was looking up at the ceiling with that serious expression in his eyes. A telltale sign that he was being summoned.

He looked at Piper, an apology in his eyes. "I'm sorry. I've gotta go."

He leaned forward to kiss her, then orbed out.

"Ugh!" Piper groaned, flopping back into her chair. "I so need an assistant."

"Come on, Piper. Come with us," Paige said, jingling her car keys in the air. "Overachiever needs a new pair of shoes!"

"Yeah. Have a little fun!" Phoebe put in.

Fun? Piper thought. *What's fun?*

She looked down at the mess of papers on the table and the floor and wondered how bad it would be, really, if she just took one day off. If she could just have one day, then maybe she could come back to all of this refreshed, with new energy. Of course she'd have to make a few phone calls . . . cancel a couple of meetings . . .

"She's gonna do it," Phoebe told Paige giddily. "I can see it in her face."

Piper was just about to open her mouth and agree when the doorbell rang. She and her sisters looked at one another quizzically. They weren't expecting anybody.

"If that's a demon or a warlock, I am going to be so pissed off," Piper said, pushing herself out of her chair. She walked through the living room, her sisters trailing behind her, and opened the door. Three burly, paint-spattered men in coveralls stood on the front step, their arms laden with paint cans, brushes, and one big ladder.

"Got a work order here for the dining room?" the man in front said, looking down at his clipboard. He chomped on a wad of gum in his mouth, then blew a large bubble.

"You have to be kidding me. *Today?*" Piper said, grasping the doorknob.

"Yep," the guy said as he stepped by her into the foyer, snapping his gum. The other two guys followed him, jostling past Piper without a word. Paige and Phoebe backed up to avoid getting hit by the ladder. The two lackeys disappeared into the living room as the man in charge took in the foyer.

"You guys have been putting me off for two weeks and then you just show up today without even *calling*?" Piper demanded, closing the door.

"Yep," he said again.

"On a *Sunday*?" Piper said, throwing her hands up in frustration.

"Dining room's in here," one of the guys called out from the doorway.

Piper looked at her sisters as the men tromped through the house and started to lay tarps all over the dining room floor.

"They're not getting any time-and-a-half week-end pay from me," Piper grumbled.

"Why don't you just tell them to come back tomorrow?" Paige asked, as Piper took a few deep breaths.

"Because if I do that, who *knows* when we'll see them again?" she said. "They were supposed to be here two weeks ago."

"So . . . now what?" Phoebe asked.

"Now I guess I'm stuck here," Piper said with a shrug. "I have to talk to them, make sure they know what they're doing."

"All right, well, we'll get home as fast as we can," Phoebe told her, reaching out to give Piper a bolstering hug.

"Yes. We will shop like the wind," Paige added. "This afternoon, we are all yours."

"Thanks, guys," Piper told them as they bustled out the door. "Have fun!"

As soon as the door was closed behind her sisters, Piper rolled her eyes to the sky and told herself to remain calm. At least things were getting done. The no-show the painters had been pulling up until now had been weighing on her mind. Now she could finally check it off her mental list.

That's it. Focus on the positive, Piper thought.

Stepping around the dining room tarps, Piper decided to take an inventory of her supplies while keeping an eye on the painters. Maybe if she dug into the back of her cabinets, she'd find she didn't have to do as much shopping as she thought. She entered the kitchen and yanked open the doors to the cabinet where she kept all the usual baking supplies—flour, sugar, baking powder, and such.

"You want the whole room in blue?" one of the painters yelled in from the dining room to Piper as she reached in to pull out some bottles of herbs.

"Blue?" she said, turning with at least ten tiny bottles pressed between her two hands. "Who said anything about blue? It's supposed to be sand."

As she whirled to face them, she saw the head painter sweep all of her paperwork across the table with his arm to make room for a paint can. Piper's face reddened.

"Hey! What're you doing? That was all organized!"

She went to put the bottles down on the island so she could run over and stop him—or at the very least freeze him—but one of the other painters knocked her arm with his elbow as he carried in one of the dining room chairs. Piper fought for balance, but half the herb and spice bottles went flying out of her hands and tumbling into Phoebe's box of charms. Piper couldn't even freeze them before they exploded open because she was still holding too many things between her fingers.

"Sorry," the painter said flatly.

"Great!" Piper said, slamming the rest of the bottles down on the counter. "Just perfect." She looked into the box and grimaced. Phoebe's carefully made charms were covered with needles of rosemary and flakes of oregano. Her sister was going to freak.

"Hey, lady. Watcha want me to do with this crap?" the head painter asked, motioning to her now completely shuffled papers. The very sight made Piper sick to her stomach.

"All right. That's it," Piper said. She reached up her hands and froze the rooms, stopping one painter in the midst of climbing a ladder, another who was mixing paint the color of the Pacific Ocean, and the leader of the group, whose mouth was hanging open in a highly unattractive manner.

Taking a deep breath, Piper attempted to calm herself, but it was no use. Her heart had transformed into a ball of stress that was pumping anxiety through her veins with every beat.

How was she going to get these guys to listen to her, get her butt to P3 to meet with the fashionistas, interview with the *Chronicle* this afternoon, *and* do the shopping and the baking?

Piper gripped the sides of the box holding Phoebe's faux wish charms and sighed.

"I wish there were two of me!" she said through her teeth, letting a bit of the anger out. She envisioned herself at the mall with her sisters, kicking back and trying on clothes and basically goofing off. It was a nice fictional picture. Too bad it was never going to happen.

Piper finally unfroze the rooms and stalked over to grab the pile of paperwork from the head painter. Then she yanked the mixing stick out of the other man's hand and snatched up the open can of paint by the handle.

"No blue, you got me?" she said. "I ordered sand and I want sand."

"Fine. Whatever you say, lady," the guy said, raising his hands in surrender.

Piper dumped the paint can and the mixing stick in the kitchen sink, grabbed her bag, and swept out of the room, the pile of paperwork under her arm. She had to check in at P3, so she was going to have to leave the painters to fend for themselves.

But if I come home and find my dining room is any color other than sand, she thought as she headed for her car, *I will* not *be responsible for my actions.*

Leo sat up straight in his soft-as-a-cloud chair in the Elders' Great Room, feeling somewhat proud. He was, after all, taking part in an event of tremendous importance in the realm of good magic, and he could sense the excitement in the warm air all around him. The chamber, which was used only for gatherings of supernatural significance, was a massive octagonal portico with gilded walls, lit by swirling white orbs that sparkled from the ceiling. Rows and rows of seating lined these walls, set up in stadium-style tiers, so that every Whitelighter could watch the proceedings on the marble floor below. The Whitelighters sat in order of seniority, those with the longest tenure along the floor, those most recently assigned charges in the highest seats. Leo was placed toward the top of the room, with a few rows above him and many rows below. He wore his white, hooded robes—the required uniform for a Whitelighter while they were "up here"—and sat with his hands folded in his lap.

On the floor below, Mariah, one of the most senior Elders, was giving a speech explaining the responsibilities of the new Elder position she and her fellows were hoping to vote into existence. This new Elder would oversee all transitioning of new ascenders from mortal to Whitelighter, a task that was now handled by an Elder named Shamus who was also in charge of training recent Whitelighters. More and more Whitelighters were being brought into the fold of late to fulfill demand. Shamus was having trouble keeping up with both their emotional well-being during the confusing ascension from mortal to immortal, *and* their practical training. Thus the need for the new Elder position.

Mariah was a commanding presence. A beautiful, tall, and imposing African American woman who had been a civil rights leader in her earthly life, she was a person who knew how to present a speech—which was the reason she'd been chosen to address the assembly, no doubt. Leo listened carefully to her argument. He had never been involved in a vote of such import, and he wanted to make sure that he made the right decision when it came time.

Suddenly a crowd of Whitelighters near the stage turned their attention to someone who was approaching Mariah on the floor. A murmur went up through the crowd, extending like a wave from row to row until it reached the Whitelighters at the very top of the Great Room. A novice—a Whitelighter who had yet to be given a charge—scurried from the outer chamber, across the marble floor to Mariah's side. Leo and the Whitelighters around him were shocked. If there was one thing they all knew, it was never to interrupt an Elder's speech, let alone a meeting in the Great Room.

"What's going on?" the Whitelighter to Leo's left whispered.

"I have no idea," Leo replied, his chest filling with trepidation.

Mariah had ceased her speech midsentence and had bent her ear toward the messenger. Her face was now lined with concern as she listened to what he had to say. Soon she straightened herself, rested a comforting hand on the novice's shoulder, and then waited for him to scurry out again before looking up at the room.

"My fellow Elders and Whitelighters, I have grave news," Mariah began, the supernatural acoustics of the room carrying her voice clearly to every ear. "It seems that the Darklighters are assembling."

Another concerned murmur went out over the crowd, this one a bit louder than the last. Darklighters were the only beings with the power to kill Whitelighters, and they did it in an insidious fashion, using poisoned arrows to ensure a slow and painful death. The idea that they might be assembling sent a palpable streak of fear through the room. Darklighters normally worked on their own—living for the simple thrill of the kill. They had no loyalty to one another and hadn't for centuries—ever since their leader, Malagon, had been banished to a middling realm by The Source. The loss of his leadership had left them at loose ends, and the Darklighters had been a purposeless, renegade lot ever since.

"Now, I'd like everyone to remain calm," Mariah said, lifting her hands to silence the assembly. "If they are planning a battle, they have picked the wrong time. We are all here, after all. And as long as we are all here, we are all safe. This realm, as we know, cannot be found or reached by a Darklighter. But once these meetings have adjourned and you return to your duties on Earth, I want you all to be on guard. Report any sightings immediately." She paused and ran her eyes over the crowd. "Whatever they are planning, they will not get away with it," she said firmly.

"Paige," Leo said under his breath as Mariah picked up her speech where she had left off. Every cell in his body tingled with dread.

"What is it, Leo?" the Whitelighter next to him whispered.

"Paige. She isn't here and she's half-Whitelighter. What if their plan isn't to attack us, but to attack the Charmed Ones?" Leo whispered back.

There was no reason for a Darklighter to have specific interest in breaking the Power of Three—they were sworn enemies to Whitelighters, not witches. But they also had never assembled like this before. Something about the situation scared Leo to his very core. He found it difficult not to squirm in the chair that had seemed so welcoming just moments ago. He had to get out of here. He had to get word to Paige and find a way to get her to safety—before it was too late.

Chapter 2

The second the Great Room meeting was adjourned for its first break, Leo made a beeline for the Elders, stepping on more than one Whitelighter's feet to get there. He hustled over to a gathering of three Elders who were whispering among themselves, noticing that Shia—one of Leo's most revered mentors—was among them. Not wishing to interrupt their conversation, Leo hovered outside the circle and cleared his throat.

"Leo!" Shia said, breaking into a smile as he noticed his younger friend. "What can we do for you?" He spread his arms wide, the bell-sleeves of his robes extended at his sides, and clapped Leo on the back.

"It's about the Darklighters," Leo said, keeping his voice low. Somehow his urgent tone still attracted the attention of a few other Elders nearby, who eyed him with concern.

"Yes. Bad business, bad business," Shia said, shaking his head. "But don't worry, Leo. What is meant to be, is meant to be. We, as Mariah said, are all safe here."

"Yes, but we're not all here," Leo said urgently. "Paige Matthews is a half-Whitelighter, remember?"

"Paige Matthews . . . Ah yes, the youngest of the Charmed sisters," Shia said, smiling nostalgically as if he were happily recalling Paige and her many exploits. Leo, a very patient person by nature, had to struggle to keep his pulse steady. He had forgotten how Shia's tendency to see the bright side could hinder conversations such as this.

"I would like permission to orb to Paige and at the very least warn her that she may be in danger," Leo said firmly.

"I don't see why she should be," Shia replied.

"Because she's a Whitelighter and a Charmed One," Leo replied. "What if the Darklighters plan to harm her in some way? We could lose the power of the Charmed Ones forever."

Not to mention the life of my sister-in-law, he added silently.

Suddenly, much to Leo's relief, Shia's expression grew grave. The implications of what Leo was saying were finally sinking in. He looked around for Mariah and beckoned her to his side with a wave of his hand.

"Give us one moment," Shia told Leo, pulling Mariah aside.

Leo waited with bated breath, his foot bouncing up and down beneath his robes. *I should just go,* he thought defiantly. *Everything takes too long around here.* But his responsible side held him back. Over the years he'd gotten himself in enough trouble with the Elders, breaking rules and ignoring orders. He could give them a few minutes to discuss in order to keep from getting on their bad side again and calling scrutiny to the Charmed Ones.

But just a few.

"Leo, Shia has explained your concerns to me," Mariah said, approaching Leo. "Our meeting is about to recommence, but we will send one of the novices to go warn the Charmed Ones."

"One of the novices?" Leo blurted, earning an admonishing glance from Mariah. Shia cleared his throat and looked down at the clouds that swirled at their feet. Leo felt his cheeks redden. "I'm sorry, but I was hoping to go myself."

"Of course you were, Leo, but we need you inside and one of the novices can easily do the job," Mariah said, resting her hand on Leo's back. "We'll send Lauren—she is one of our most promising young Whitelighters. Will that satisfy you?"

No, Leo thought. *I need to see Paige. No one but me can make her understand how real this threat is.*

But under Mariah's penetrating gaze, he managed to keep his mouth shut. He didn't want to rock the boat any more than he needed to, and Mariah was right. Lauren would do the job admirably. She was one of the most eager students they had and had made the transition from the mortal plane with self-assured ease.

"Yes," he said finally, swallowing his pride. "Lauren will be fine. Thank you."

"Thank you for bringing the problem to our attention," Shia said, patting Leo's shoulder.

He began to usher Leo back into the Great Room with the other Whitelighters and Elders, but Leo purposely shuffled slowly, watching from the corner of his eye as Mariah spoke with Lauren, the towheaded young novice who was going to be entrusted with Paige's safety. Leo saw Lauren nod resolutely, her eyes filled with resolve. He watched her orb out.

Just make sure she understands the gravity of the situation, Leo willed Lauren silently.

The Darklighters were up to something, and Leo knew he wouldn't feel quite comfortable until he saw his whole family together again.

"Hey! What're you doing?" Piper called out, hustling across the dance floor at P3.

A couple of men she'd never seen before were standing on step stools, removing the velvet curtains that surrounded the VIP alcoves. The music was cranked up to its highest decibel, and the club was buzzing with fashionistas and construction workers—two groups of people who did not visually mesh. Over by the stage, the designer

Rinaldo and his assistant Marsha were watching a few leggy models strut around to the bass beat pounding through the speakers. Rinaldo was wearing what appeared to be a purple bathrobe and had a black beret pulled over his bald head. Criticisms spewed from his mouth at a loud volume. "Walk like a girl! Pout like you mean it! Stand up straight, honey! This isn't a Cro-Magnon show!"

Trying not to let his nasal voice distract and irritate her, Piper grabbed one of the curtains from an overall-wearing worker who was about to drop it on the floor.

"I *said*, what are you doing?" she snapped at him.

"My job," the guy answered, shouting to be heard over the music. "Who are you?"

"Oh, just the person who owns this place," Piper yelled. "You're destroying my VIP area."

A couple of other men gathered up the plush pillows and cushions from the built-in benches within the alcoves and tossed them into huge laundry bins. The velvet-cube tables had already been removed, and Piper didn't even want to *think* of where these guys might have put them.

"Hey. Douglas told me these things needed to come down," the worker said, raising his calloused hands. "Your beef is with him."

"Douglas?" Piper asked, folding the thick, heavy curtain awkwardly over her arm. "Who's Douglas?"

"I am."

Piper turned at the sound of a deep, British-accent-tinged voice behind her. A tall man in an impeccable suit eyed her with a superior smirk on his face. His brown hair was perfectly tousled, and he held a leather folder in both hands. He gave her the once-over with a flick of his eyes and didn't appear to be all that impressed.

"Douglas Brittany. I'm Rinaldo's business manager. And you are?" he asked, arching his eyebrows. Piper noticed that he had intensely beautiful green eyes—which were totally wasted on someone as obviously obnoxious as himself.

"Piper Halliwell," she shouted to be heard over the music. "Owner of P3? The club in which you're currently standing? And your workers seem to be under the impression that they can take apart my VIP area."

"All of this is going to have to come out to accommodate the seating," Douglas said, waving his arm around and looking at her like she was just a nuisance and not the person he had to answer to. "We have to break down these divider walls to open up the space."

"Break down the *walls*? Are you insane?" Piper demanded, flushing. "I didn't authorize that."

"Well, it needs to be done," Douglas replied. To him this was clearly no big deal. He probably walked into people's places of business every day, destroyed them, and walked right out again, with no remorse.

Piper breathed in and out deliberately, restraining herself from blowing up her first-ever human. "I thought the seating was going to be over by the stage," she shouted.

This was no way to have a civil conversation—Piper's head was starting to pound in time to the music. Over in the DJ booth, Piper's new DJ, Carlita, who had been asked to come in to help with Rinaldo's rehearsal, was dancing around as she spun the tunes. Her pink hair was a blur as she moved back and forth, holding one headphone to her ear.

"Can we cut it, please?" Piper practically screamed at the girl, her head exploding with pain.

Carlita nodded and flashed a thumbs-up before cutting the beat short. The lack of music made the sound of the hammering and buzz saws over by the stage more obvious, but the relative silence was lovely and Piper sighed, her eardrums relieved. At least one person in this place still listened to her. Of course, the sudden absence of electronica caught Rinaldo's attention as well, and he glanced around in obvious irritation. Piper wondered if Rinaldo listened to that stuff 24/7, but she didn't care. She was dealing with Mr. Brit-Snob at the moment.

"There's no way we'll fit everyone over there," Douglas said, folding his leather binder against his chest. "Do you have any idea how many people one of Rinaldo's shows will bring in?"

Could you be any more condescending? Piper wondered.

She placed the heavy curtain on top of the bar and straightened her jacket, lifting her chin slightly to let Douglas know she was not intimidated. He was clearly one of those people who was used to others kowtowing in front of him. Little did he know that a Charmed One never kowtowed.

At least, not anymore. There was a point in time, when Piper had first started working in the restaurant business, when she'd been unable to stand up for herself, but over the years that had changed. It had changed in a big way.

"I am sure that Rinaldo's shows attract many, *many* people, which is why I agreed to host this thing in the first place. And my club can handle many, many people," Piper told Douglas firmly, staring him down. "You are not going to demolish my VIP alcoves."

"Is there a problem over here?" Rinaldo asked, scurrying over from the stage area, followed by his assistant and a few other random entourage types. "Piper! How lovely to see you!" He double air-kissed her, the toxic cloud of his personally concocted cologne filling her lungs and nearly choking her. The stores had pulled that crap from the shelves months ago, but Rinaldo still insisted on wearing it.

Mental note: Hold your breath around Rinaldo, Piper thought, trying not to look too disgusted.

"No. No problem," Douglas said haughtily.

"Yes. There is," Piper put in. "I've already

agreed to adding a catwalk extension to the stage and to putting softer lighting in that area of the club, but I never said you could renovate my VIP area."

"Well, Piper, we're going to have to take everything out anyway, if we're going to put in the new floor," Marsha said, joining the pow-wow. She flicked an invisible speck from the sleeve of her black cashmere sweater.

"New *floor*?" Piper asked. Who did these people think they were?

"You don't expect me to invite my friends and colleagues to drag their Jimmy Choos across *this*, do you?" Rinaldo said, grimacing at the admittedly ratty floor. It was stained in places, torn up slightly in others, and sported a few random sticky spots that even the most powerful of industrial cleaners had not been able to cut through. Rinaldo lifted his hands toward his chest as he regarded it, as if his fingers were all too close to the atrocity.

"It's a dance club. The floor gets spilled on and danced on. That's what it's for," Piper said.

"Look, *Piper,* is it?" Douglas sneered, the sardonic smirk in place. "I'm sure you're very good at what you do, but so are we. And this place is inadequate in its current state."

Piper's face reddened in fury. "Well then, maybe you need to find another place!" she said. "Someplace that *is* adequate."

There was no way she was going to stand here

while they insulted her club. Especially not when she had a thousand other things she could be doing. Useful things. She grabbed her bag and turned to stalk out, but halfway across the room she realized they should be the ones to leave. They were the interlopers, the insulters, the guests in *her* place of business. Piper was turning around to say just that when Marsha caught up to her, red curls bouncing around her face as she struggled to jog in her stiletto-heeled boots.

"Piper, listen. Rinaldo really wants to have his show here," Marsha said placatingly, resting her hand on Piper's arm. Her long red nails glinted in the lights from overhead. "Isn't there any way we can compromise?"

A sudden flash caught Piper's attention. Up on the stage, a group of leggy models posed for a photographer while a seamstress took the measurements of a pin-up–worthy girl in the corner. A few other fashion lackeys held up scanty outfits, studying them and making notes on their clipboards. Piper sighed, remembering why she had agreed to do this in the first place—the models would bring in male gawkers and the clothes would bring in female gawkers, all of whom would buy drinks from Piper's bar. It was good for business all around. But still, she wasn't going to give in on *everything*.

"We can talk about the floor," Piper said finally. "But you guys are not messing with my VIP area."

"Fine," Marsha said, laughing nervously. It was so weird how all these people she hadn't known a week ago acted like they were her best friends. "I'm sure that'll be . . . fine." As they started back toward the others, Marsha hooked her arm through Piper's. "Have you ever thought about modeling? I bet I could get Rinaldo to work you into the show . . . if you were willing to reconsider—"

"No way," Piper said, shaking her head. Not only would she feel like the runt of the model litter, at barely five feet tall, but also there was absolutely no way she was going to get up there and strut around in front of hundreds of people. It was like her personal version of hell.

"But Rinaldo's new line would look just *fabulous* on you," Marsha attempted, her voice dripping with honey.

"Nice try," Piper said. "But that is not the way to this girl's heart."

She walked purposefully over to the bar, picked up the velvet curtain, and handed it to the worker who was still standing up on his stepladder.

"You, put this back up," she said. Then she turned to Douglas. "And you, get some estimates for the floor and we'll talk about it later."

Douglas's expression grew indignant. "I don't take orders from—"

"Oh, Piper! I'm so *pleased*!" Rinaldo said, interrupting Douglas to air-kiss Piper yet again.

This time she remembered not to inhale. "I'm sure we can work something out," he added, sliding his eyes toward his business manager with an admonishing look.

"I'm sure we can," Piper replied with a forced smile. "Now I've got a few other things to take care of, but I'll be back this afternoon to check in."

"Fabulous! We'll see you then!" Rinaldo called out, waggling his fingers after Piper as she swept up the stairs. She hadn't even gotten to the door yet when the music started up again, shaking the steps beneath her.

Once outside in the fresh air, Piper started to feel rather good about putting Douglas in his place and taking charge of things. Plus she had checked in on P3—a task she could now mark off her to-do list. Maybe there was hope for her crazy day yet.

"Do you think we should call Piper?" Paige asked from outside the dressing room where Phoebe was trying on clothes.

"Why?" Phoebe replied, as she stepped into a gray skirt. She was starting to perspire from throwing on and off a million outfits, none of which had seemed remotely right.

"I don't know. She was kind of stressed this morning," Paige said. "I'm a little worried about her."

"Please, that's just Piper," Phoebe told Paige as she secured the side button on the skirt. "If there's anyone who can handle all that stuff, it's her."

"I guess," Paige said. "I just wish she would take a little time to unwind every once in a while. All work and no play . . . well . . . you know."

"I agree with you there. Piper is long overdue for some R&R," Phoebe said, pulling on the matching jacket. "Maybe when this fashion show thing is over."

"Yeah. Maybe," Paige replied. "I'm gonna go look around."

"'Kay!"

Phoebe turned in front of the three-way dressing room mirror, trying to find at least one attractive angle, but it was no use. Responsible gray was just not a Phoebe Halliwell hue. Was she the only woman in the world who wanted to look alluring in the workplace? On a normal day Phoebe wore anything she wanted—sporting colors and cuts that usually attracted a lot of attention in the office. But Elise had requested she tone it down a bit for this advertising meeting, and she wouldn't have asked unless it was important. Phoebe was pretty much stuck.

"Okay, she said tone it down, not dress for a funeral," Phoebe whispered under her breath. She ripped off the gray jacket and replaced it on its hanger. There just had to be a happy medium.

"Phoebe, you have to try this on!" Paige said from outside the spacious cubicle. An extremely low-cut red dress appeared over the top of the slatted door, and Phoebe, who had started shimmying out of the itchy pencil skirt, paused. This dress was *killer*.

"Ooooh," Phoebe cooed, taking the dress from Paige's hand and letting the skirt fall down around her ankles. "I love this. I love this so much I want to marry it. . . ."

"Try it on!" Paige told her.

Phoebe held the dress up to her. She smiled when she saw the color against her skin. Now *this* was a Halliwell hue. And the dress was definitely supermodel-worthy.

"Paige, I don't think Elise would appreciate me showing up for the meeting in this," Phoebe said, nevertheless stepping out of the wool crepe skirt and into the luscious red fabric. She slipped the thin straps over her shoulders, zipped up the back, and checked her reflection in the mirror. "Oh yeah," she said, striking a pose.

"Let me see!" Paige called out.

Phoebe opened the dressing room door and placed her hands on her hips, arching her back and giving her sister a perfect pout. Paige's mouth dropped open, and a guy shopping with his girlfriend on the other side of the store almost fell over. Phoebe giggled and turned to look at her reflection again. She couldn't take her eyes off herself.

"You need that dress," Paige said, stepping up behind her to look at her in the mirror.

"I really think I do," Phoebe said giddily,

checking the price tag. "It'll cost three months' pay and I have no place to wear it, but I really think I need it."

Paige's cell phone rang, and Phoebe twirled in front of the mirror. Now *this* ensemble looked good from *every* angle. Of course, it was going to require a new pair of shoes. . . .

"Hey, Piper!" Paige said into the phone. "How's it going?"

Phoebe watched her sister in the mirror, hoping her face wouldn't do that creasing thing it did whenever there was bad news. Instead, Paige's eyes widened and her face lit up.

"You're here?" she said, glancing at Phoebe. "Yeah. We're still shopping. We're at Heartly's. Okay . . . cool!" She folded her phone closed and dropped it back into her bag. "She's on her way!"

"You're kidding!" Phoebe said, impressed. "What a rebel."

"I know!" Paige replied, leaning on top of a display of blouses. "You better get out of that dress, though. She'll kill us if she sees we were wasting time. She'll probably send us directly to the grocery store—do not pass Go, do not collect gorgeous red dress."

"Good point," Phoebe said, lifting the sides of the skirt. She was about to disappear into the safety of her cubicle, but it was already too late.

"Phoebe!" Piper's admonishing voice called across the store.

"That was quick," Paige said under her breath as Phoebe cringed. She stood up straight and waited as her sister crossed the store, steeling herself for the lecture that was about to come. But much to Phoebe's surprise, Piper's expression was one of pure delight, not disgust. Maybe she'd misjudged that tone in her voice.

"*Where* did you find that dress?" Piper said, looking Phoebe up and down.

Phoebe glanced at Paige, confused. "Um . . . Paige found it for me," she said, deflecting the blame.

"Omigod, I *have* to try that on," Piper said, reaching out and fingering the lush fabric. "Leo would die."

"You want to try *this* on?" Phoebe said, pointing at herself with both hands and wondering if Piper had hit her head on the way over. Her sister wasn't exactly one for showing off the goods. It wasn't that she didn't have them, as Phoebe had been pointing out their entire lives, it was just that she wasn't the type to flaunt them.

"Yes! Get in there and get out of it!" Piper said, giving Phoebe a little push toward the dressing room. Phoebe didn't move. She and Paige watched Piper with matching dumbfounded expressions. "What?" Piper asked. "You're the ones who told me I had to start having fun." She grabbed a black, sequined minidress from a nearby sale rack and snagged the dressing room next to Phoebe's. "Let's have a little fun!" she trilled, slamming the door behind her.

Phoebe laughed, surprised but happy to see her sister in such a lighthearted state. She was still wondering where it had come from, but she wasn't about to press the issue. All she could think about was enjoying it while it lasted.

"I'll go get more dresses!" Paige said with a shrug.

"And I'll get out of this one!" Phoebe added, thinking if it looked good on all of them, it would be great to split the cost and share it.

"Get me something in purple!" Piper called out. "I like purple!"

Phoebe smiled to herself in her dressing room, shaking her head at her reflection as she slipped out of the red dress and handed it under the divider to Piper. She wasn't sure if her sister was having a breakdown or just blowing off a little steam, but either way, she liked this new attitude. The last time Piper had kicked back and had a little fun . . . well . . . Phoebe couldn't even remember it.

A few minutes later a wad of hangers and beading and straps and sequins appeared over the top of Phoebe's dressing room door. Phoebe hung all the gowns on the hook to her right, covering up the responsible outfits she'd already passed on. At that moment Piper must have slipped into the red dress, because she shouted out, "This is to die for!" from the next room.

"I got some for me, too!" Paige said, slamming into the room to Phoebe's left. Phoebe stepped into a green, bias-cut number and waited, swishing the skirt back and forth.

"Everyone ready?" she said a few minutes later.

"I am!" Piper called out, her voice excited and high-pitched.

"Me too!" Paige said.

"Okay, on the count of three, we walk out," Phoebe announced giddily. "One, two, three!"

Let the fashion show begin!

"I still can't believe you bought that jacket," Paige said to Piper with a grin, opening the door to the Manor that afternoon and letting her sister in first.

Paige had just experienced her first-ever shopping spree with both her sisters and was feeling a little giddy over the whole scenario. They had spent an hour trying on things they knew they'd never wear, striking poses, laughing like teenagers, and ever-so-slightly irritating the salespeople. Growing up, Paige had never had sisters to share things like that with, and now she felt as if she were making up for lost time. She hadn't even bought anything for herself—she'd simply enjoyed the company.

"What? It's not me?" Piper asked. She paused in front of the mirror in the front hall and ran her hand down the soft, cream-colored leather sleeve, tossing her hair back and admiring her reflection.

"No. The color is totally you and you're definitely workin' the leather. It's just so impractical. That's what's not-Piper about it," Paige explained as Phoebe walked in, swinging her many shopping bags. "One drop of anything and that jacket is done for."

"Which is why you'll never be borrowing it," Piper said with a hint of sarcasm.

"Ha ha," Paige replied, rolling her eyes as she slipped off her own long denim coat.

"She's right though, Piper," Phoebe replied, eyeing the new purchase. "You sure you want to take on the added responsibility of caring for such a luscious garment?" She made a sexy face in the mirror on the word *luscious* and Paige had to laugh.

"I don't care," Piper said. "For once in my life, I'm going with style before substance."

"You go, girl," Phoebe said, dropping her bags at the foot of the stairs and stretching as she stood up straight. "What do you guys want to do now? I'm starving!"

Paige was about to suggest they take a load off and order in when the doorknob started to turn and they heard bustling on the other side of the glass. Glancing at her sisters, Paige backed up slightly, concerned. They were all home, and Leo didn't use the door.

Before they even had a chance to wonder what they were about to see, the door burst open and they were met with, not an enraged demon, but an armload full of four brown shopping bags. As the carrier staggered into the room under their weight, Paige could have sworn she was looking at Piper's outstretched hand trying to sightlessly put down her keys on the table.

But that, of course, wasn't possible. Piper was standing right next to her.

"Little help here, please?"

Okay, apparently it is *possible,* Paige thought, her stomach dropping down to her toes. It was Piper's voice coming from behind all those bags, and before any one of them could react, it was Piper's head that stuck out from around the side of the packages, a desperate look on her face as she attempted to balance them all.

Paige's heart hit her throat. "What the—"

"Who the hell are you?" the Piper in the leather jacket said, causing the Piper with the bags to drop them all over the floor. A canister of baking powder rolled into the dining room and boxes and plastic bags tumbled out at their feet, but no one took notice.

"Who am I?" the new Piper replied, her brow furrowing. "Who the hell are you?"

Phoebe took a few steps away from one Piper, toward the other, and looked back and forth between the two of them. Time seemed to stop as all *four* sisters stared at each other, waiting for someone to come up with an explanation. Phoebe reached out and took each Piper's left hand, looking down at their identical wedding bands, their identical gnarled cuticles, the identical freckle on the back of each of their wrists.

"Oh . . . my . . . God," Phoebe said, her shoulders up by her ears.

"Get out of my body!" both Pipers shouted at the exact same time, in the exact same voice.

"Well," Paige said, crossing her arms over her chest and arching one eyebrow. "This is new."

Chapter 3

"She's a warlock! She's a warlock and she stole my body!" the Piper near the stairs shouted, pointing both hands at her double.

"Please! *You're* obviously a warlock," the other Piper replied with an indignant toss of her head. "I would never wear a jacket like that!"

"Hey! This jacket is an *investment*!"

"Right. One sun shower and that thing is toast."

"All right! That's it!"

The Piper in the leather jacket raised her hands to blow up her doppelganger, but Paige launched forward and grabbed her wrists, pulling her arms down to her sides and holding them there. Phoebe, meanwhile, jumped in front of the other Piper to keep her from doing the same thing.

"Don't!" Phoebe said, slapping Piper's hand

as she tried to reach around Phoebe and vanquish her new twin. "Don't!" Phoebe repeated, slapping the other hand. She sighed, exasperated. "Do I have to get my handcuffs?"

"You have handcuffs?" both Pipers asked, their eyebrows shooting up.

Phoebe had the sudden sensation that she was standing in the middle of the mirror room in a carnival funhouse, only instead of being surrounded by images of *herself*, she was surrounded by Pipers.

"Okay, everybody just . . . calm . . . down!" Phoebe said, her eyes wide. She was now holding on to her Piper's wrists, just as Paige was doing to the other Piper. "There has to be a reasonable explanation for this."

"Yes, there is!" leather-sporting Piper said, struggling to free her hands from Paige's grip. "She's an imposter. You guys know I'm me. We just spent the whole afternoon together."

"Ha! That proves you're *not* me!" the other Piper shot back, tossing her hair. She yanked her hands away from Phoebe with one swift tug and stuffed them under her arms before Phoebe could grab them back. "You guys *know* I had a million things to do today. You really think I'd blow all that off for a little shopping spree?"

"That *was* a little weird," Phoebe said, eyeing the Piper near the stairs warily. This was all just too intense. How could she be standing next to Piper while looking at Piper from across the room? Phoebe's mind was practically spinning.

"Okay, people! I think I have an idea," Paige announced. She seemed to be taking the situation rather well. "There is an easy way to solve this."

"Please share," Phoebe implored.

"We just have to do that thing where we ask them questions only Piper would know the answers to," Paige said, lifting one shoulder casually even as she still clenched Piper's wrists. "It always works in the movies."

"Oh come on," one of the Pipers said. "Just let me blow her up."

"Piper!" Phoebe admonished.

"What?" they both snapped.

Phoebe brought her hands to her head and paced back and forth between them, trying to get a handle on the situation. The only sounds in the house were the ticking of the grandfather clock and the scuffing of Phoebe's shoes against the hardwood floor.

"Okay, from this point on, you're Piper One," Phoebe said, pointing at the Piper near the door. "And you're Piper Two," she added, pointing at the Piper in the leather jacket.

"I don't see why I have to be Two—"

"Zip it!" Phoebe said, raising her hand. "Paige, you can let go of her."

"You sure?" Paige asked uncertainly.

"Don't blow anything up until we figure this out," Phoebe told Piper Two firmly, raising a warning finger.

"Fine," Piper Two replied, rolling her eyes to the sky.

Paige and Phoebe stepped up together and watched the two Pipers survey each other. The resemblance was uncanny. Aside from the new leather jacket, they were both wearing the same exact outfit Piper had been sporting that morning—hip-hugging blue jeans and a long-sleeved black T-shirt. They each wore Piper's favorite beaded cuff bracelet on one arm, a watch on the other, and the very same wedding ring. There could have been a mirror in front of one of them.

This is very disturbing, Phoebe thought. Prue had tripled herself once a few years back, but they had all been there and watched it happen. Plus, all the Prues had worked together from the start. Each of these two Pipers seemed to be extremely confused by the other one's presence.

"Okay, let's go with your plan," Phoebe said under her breath. "What can we ask her?"

"Um . . . okay . . . what's your husband's name?" Paige asked.

"Leo Wyatt," the Pipers replied at the same time in a tone that said the question was far too easy.

"Okay, what was the name of the boyfriend you *claim* I stole from you in middle school?" Phoebe asked, clasping her hands together and shifting her weight from foot to foot.

"Billy Wilson," the Pipers both said simultaneously.

"And you did steal him," Piper Two added.

"Blatantly," Piper One said.

"Oh! I got one!" Paige exclaimed, hopping slightly. "Where did you first meet me?"

"Right here," the Pipers replied in unison. "The night you became a witch."

"What was the name of the first warlock we vanquished?" Phoebe put in.

"Jeremy."

"Where did you hide your diary when we were little?"

"Under the flowerpot in the backyard."

"How did our mother die?"

"Drowning."

The more questions they both got right, the more the two Pipers fumed at each other. It was a silent fuming, but it was practically palpable. Their nostrils flared and they started to pace back and forth across from each other like a pair of twin lionesses. Finally they stopped, turned, and glared at Phoebe and Paige, arms crossed over their chests.

"This isn't working," they said together.

Paige laughed under her breath. "Leo is going to *love* this."

"This is no time for jokes," Phoebe said, rolling her eyes. She walked into the solarium and sat down hard on the edge of the couch, thinking. "I've got it!" she said, lifting her head and looking at Piper One. "You, try to freeze her."

"Gladly," Piper One said, lifting her hands.

Piper Two opened her mouth in indignation. "Why does *she* get to freeze *me*?"

But Piper One had already tried, and Piper Two had continued talking. The freeze had failed. They all knew there was only one explanation for that.

"She didn't freeze!" Paige said. "She's immune to our powers. That means she's a good witch!"

"I told you!" Piper Two said. She lifted her arms to freeze Piper One—and again, nothing happened.

"They're both good witches," Phoebe said, a foreboding cloud surrounding her heart. There was some serious magic going on here, and she had no idea how it had happened. She didn't, in fact, care how it had happened. All she wanted to know was who her real sister was.

"This isn't possible," Piper One said, looking around at her sisters. "How is this possible?"

"I don't know. But don't worry, we'll figure it out," Paige said, reaching out and rubbing Piper Two's arm.

"Hey, she's the one who's worried," Piper Two said indignantly. "I *know* we'll figure it out."

Piper One shot Piper Two a snotty, nose-scrunched look, and Phoebe sighed, wondering where to begin. Her eyes traveled to the open kitchen, probably to avoid the oddity of what was before her, and she noticed her box of wish charms lying next to the extra set of chairs the painters had moved out of the dining room. Phoebe's eyes narrowed when she saw the mess of herbs that covered her charms.

"Wait a minute," Phoebe said, walking over to the box. "What happened to my wish charms?"

"Oh yeah, that's what we should be focusing on right now," Piper Two said testily.

"Right, sorry, Phoebe," Piper One put in. "This painter knocked into me and I spilled some herbs in there. I'll clean them up for you later."

Phoebe's stomach did that coiling thing it did whenever she was on to something a little bit exciting and a little bit scary. Was it even possible? She'd specifically left out key ingredients so that there would be no chance of them actually working. . . .

"Piper, you didn't happen to make a wish after you trashed my wish charms, did you?" Phoebe asked, looking from one of them to the other.

The Pipers locked eyes with each other, their faces registering realization, then resignation.

"Oh, God," Piper One said.

"The wish!" Piper Two cried.

"Here's the list of ingredients I used in the wish charms," Phoebe said, walking into the cluttered kitchen where Paige was already checking over the bottles Piper had dropped into the cardboard box. Next door, the half-painted dining room was quiet. The painters had apparently decided to go on their lunch break before the sisters had returned home, which was fine by Paige. She wanted to get this sorted out before any mortals had a chance to get confused by all the insanity.

Piper One and Piper Two sat at the kitchen table, staring unblinkingly at each other. Every once in a while one of them would tilt her head to one side, and the other Piper would mirror her. It was starting to freak Paige out.

"Could you guys stop with the mirror game?" Paige asked, tightening the top on the rosemary bottle. "And stop staring at each other. It's creepy."

"Sorry," Piper Two said. "It's just . . . so cool."

"Yeah," Piper One put in. "Do you really think I doubled myself?"

Paige, the resident potion specialist, scanned down Phoebe's list of ingredients and looked over the bottles she had lined up on the counter. There was no doubt about it. Piper had mistakenly mixed herself up one heck of a potent concoction.

"Yep," Paige said, standing up straight. "I think you just might have. In fact, I think we might need to add this recipe to the Book of Shadows."

"Or destroy it," Phoebe suggested, hand on her hip. "I think this definitely falls under the heading of 'Be careful what you wish for.'"

"Okay, so what do we do?" Piper One asked. "How do we reverse it?"

"I'm not sure," Paige said, biting her lip. "I don't really know what reversing it is going to . . . you know . . . do to you guys."

The two Pipers looked at each other, disturbed, and Paige swallowed. Technically, if Piper had doubled herself, both Pipers *were* Piper. It was a little tough to wrap the brain around, but there it was. Reversing the spell might leave them with only one Piper, but what if doing that was akin to killing one of them?

"Maybe we should call Leo," Phoebe suggested, sounding tense.

"Leo!" All four sisters shouted at the same time.

They waited in silence, looking at the ceiling, until it became obvious that he wasn't going to show.

"That's a little weird," Paige said.

"Well, he told us he was going to be out of commission for a while," Piper One said. "And technically none of us is hurt. . . ."

"Okay, I hate to suggest the obvious, since it rarely ever works, but what if you guys try wishing that there were just one of you?" Phoebe suggested, bringing the box of wish charms over to the table. "Maybe a simple wish will reverse a simple wish."

The two Pipers regarded each other and then

each shrugged one shoulder. "Worth a try," Piper Two said.

From either side of the table, the Pipers reached out and grasped the sides of the box, just as Piper had done earlier in her fit of impatience.

"Ready?" Piper One said.

Paige held her breath and hoped for the best.

"Ready," Piper Two replied.

"I wish there were one of me!" both Pipers shouted at the same time, closing their eyes.

Paige winced, waiting for some swirl of light or big explosion or blast of wind—phenomena she'd become accustomed to since learning about her Charmed destiny. But nothing happened. The two Pipers were still there.

"So much for that," Piper Two said, crossing her arms over her chest.

"I knew it was too easy," Phoebe said. "Why can't we live in a world where a wish just reverses a wish?"

"I hate to say it, but maybe it's a personal gain thing," Paige said.

"But I didn't even do this on purpose!" Piper Two protested.

"Yeah, but it was still a selfish wish," Piper One reminded her. "Paige might be right. We may be stuck like this as some sort of punishment."

"Well, that bites," Piper Two said.

The other three sisters looked at her, surprised.

Looks like Piper Two has a temper, Paige thought.

"Well, I'm going to go check the Book of Shadows," Paige said, grabbing Phoebe's list of ingredients along with a pen to write down the herbs and spices Piper had added. "It may take a while, though."

"I'll help," Phoebe said, grabbing up the box of wish charms to take with them. She looked over at the Pipers, her brow creasing. "You two just . . . sit tight."

"Yeah," Paige told them confidently. "We'll figure something out."

As she turned to leave the room, a chill of foreboding skittered down her back—a chill she'd long since grown to associate with uncertainty. There was something about this magical blip that was different from all the other ones they'd suffered. Piper had created a whole new *person.* That was serious. It seemed to Paige to be pretty high up there on the messing-with-stuff-that-shouldn't-be-messed-with scale.

Paige was about to climb the stairs when she heard what sounded like a scuffle coming from outside the front door. She and Phoebe both froze.

"Did you hear that?" Paige asked, holding her breath.

There was a sudden scream from the other side of the glass. A female scream.

"I heard *that,*" Phoebe said, rushing for the door.

"Piper . . . *s*!" Paige called out, adding the plural as an afterthought. Her heart pounded as she rushed up behind Phoebe, wondering what kind of demon was on their tails this time.

Neither Paige nor Phoebe could have been prepared for the sight that greeted them on the other side of the door. A blond girl of about eighteen, wearing a long white dress, lay on the doorstep, an arrow sticking out of her chest. Hovering above her was a Darklighter, still grinning with triumph over the kill. His blond hair stuck out in all directions, and he was missing a few front teeth.

"Paige, get back!" Phoebe shouted.

Paige saw her life flash before her as the Darklighter locked eyes with her. She started to back away, not nearly fast enough, but the Darklighter merely laughed, tipping his head back slightly. At that moment both Pipers ran up behind Paige and lifted their hands to blow the thing to Kingdom Come, but he disappeared in a puff of black smoke before they ever got the chance.

"He didn't kill me," Paige said, slightly dazed.

"You guys! Help me! She's still alive!" Phoebe said. She bent over the girl and tried to lift her up, but the Whitelighter cried out in pain. Paige dropped down and reached for the arrow, but Phoebe grasped her hands to stop her.

"Don't! It's poisonous to you!" she said urgently.

Paige swallowed hard. How could she have been so careless? A little near-death experience shouldn't have thrown her so badly. It wasn't as if she hadn't had them before. Phoebe removed the arrow, causing the girl to groan miserably, then the four sisters carried her inside and laid her down on the couch in the parlor.

"Can you heal her, Paige?" Phoebe asked, backing away from the Whitelighter.

"I can try," Paige said. She knelt down next to the girl and placed her hands over the wound, but the girl reached up and touched her wrist. Her grip was very weak.

"It's . . . too . . . late," she said, breathing sporadically. "The poison was too close . . . to . . . my heart. Don't have much time. Have to . . . warn you."

"Warn us? About what?" Paige asked, her skin sizzling.

"The Elders . . . they sent me to tell you . . ." The girl paused and took a few gulps of air. "The Darklighters are assembling. They're coming . . . for . . . you."

Paige felt as if someone had lowered her into a bucket of ice. The Darklighters assembling and coming for her? That did not sound like a party.

Suddenly the girl coughed, her whole body going into spasm. Paige recalled herself and placed her hands over the wound again, trying to heal her, but because Paige was only part Whitelighter, she had no real healing powers of her own. She needed to channel the dying girl's powers and redirect them back into her, but the girl was too far gone. As she, Phoebe, and the two Pipers watched, the Whitelighter closed her eyes for the last time. They never even learned her name.

Paige stood up very slowly, tears burning in her eyes. "She was so young," she said, looking around at her sisters.

"It's okay, Paige," Piper One said, touching her arm. "You did everything you could."

"What about the warning?" Piper Two said. "An army of Darklighters coming for Paige? I don't like the sound of that."

"I don't know," Phoebe said, pulling a blanket off the back of the couch and covering the girl with it. She turned to her sisters, her brow furrowed. "It doesn't really make sense. That Darklighter was standing right there and Paige was fully exposed. He didn't even make a move."

"So maybe the girl was wrong?" Paige said hopefully. "Maybe they're not after me?"

"Why did they send her?" Piper One asked, pacing the room. "If Paige's life was in danger, why not let Leo come and explain everything?"

"They would have if they thought it was a big enough threat, right?" Paige put in, still clinging to the possibility that the Whitelighter had been wrong. That there wasn't a battalion of poison-toting warriors waiting to bust down her door.

"Who knows?" Piper Two said. "It's *Them*."

There wasn't much love lost between Piper and the Elders after the months they'd spent keeping Piper and Leo apart. It had once been strictly forbidden for a Whitelighter and a witch to be together, and the Elders had done everything They could to try to quash Leo and Piper's love. But when They had seen Piper fight tirelessly for the greater good, not to mention the fact that the couple wasn't about to give up, They had finally allowed them to marry.

"All we know is, that Darklighter tried to stop her from warning us about something," Phoebe said. "For now, we've got to at least be prepared for the worst. We're going to have to watch Paige's back."

"Yes, please," Paige said, walking over to Phoebe, who wrapped one arm around her comfortingly.

"As if we didn't have enough to deal with," Piper Two said under her breath.

"Okay, let's get back to the task at hand," Phoebe said, clapping her hands together. "We need to get to the Book of Shadows and see if we can find a way to fix this wish thing. No offense, but I trust the Power of Three more than the Power of Four, and with this Darklighter thing, we might need it."

"What about the girl?" Paige asked.

Before anyone could answer, some white orbs appeared above the girl's body and swirled up into the air, disappearing through the ceiling. The blanket that had covered her retained the shape of her body for a split second, then collapsed to the couch.

Phoebe smiled sadly, watching the spot where the orbs had disappeared. "I think she's moved on to a better place," she said. "Come on. Let's go check the Book."

Paige followed Phoebe, wondering if when she died, her body would just disappear in an orb-fest like that. She kind of liked the idea. If she was going to go, that seemed like a pleasant way. She just hoped it wasn't going to be any time soon. It wasn't until she was halfway up the steps that she realized the Pipers weren't following.

"You guys coming?" she called, leaning over the banister.

"Be right there!" they called back in the exact same tone.

Paige shook her head and kept walking. Piper in stereo was going to take some getting used to. As was the idea that a force of Darklighters might pop in at any moment and take her out.

This day was going to be one for the record books.

"Know what I'm thinking?" Piper Two asked Piper One mischievously, lowering herself onto the couch. She spoke quietly, listening to her sisters' footsteps as they climbed both sets of stairs to the attic.

Piper One blinked. "Oddly, no. You'd think I would since we share the same brain," she replied as she sat next to her double.

"Well *I'm* thinking I have way too much to do to deal with *this*," Piper Two said, waving her hand back and forth between the two of them.

"I know," Piper One said with a sigh. "But I think that even with everything that's going on, fixing *this* problem has to be our first priority."

"Absolutely! Of course! But you heard what Paige said. It's going to take a while," Piper Two argued. "So in the meantime, why don't we take this doppelganger thing out for a spin and see what it can do?"

"What do you mean, exactly?" Piper One asked, shifting in her seat.

"I mean, the painters are going to come back from their break eventually," Piper Two said, glancing toward the dining room, which was in total shambles. "There's all that baking to do . . ."

"And the interview this afternoon . . . ," Piper One put in, finally catching on.

"And we have to keep an eye on P3 . . ."

"And someone has to be here to make sure nothing happens to Paige . . ."

"And we suddenly have the capacity to take care of everything without breaking a sweat," Piper Two said.

"I don't know . . . ," Piper One replied, glancing toward the stairs. She knew what her sisters would say if they were here right now. There was too much risk involved in putting two Pipers out in the world. What if someone saw them? What if something went wrong?

"Come on! We might as well take advantage of this while we can!" Piper Two prodded her.

"Well, maybe if one of us stays here so we can't be spotted . . . ," Piper One said. "It would be nice to actually get some things done."

"Exactly," Piper Two added. "Why let a good thing go to waste? This was what I wanted, right? Two of me."

"Maybe this actually happened for a reason," Piper One said slowly. "Maybe you were supposed to be here to help me out."

"Or *you* were supposed to be here to help *me* out," Piper Two put in, raising her eyebrows.

"Of course! Whatever," Piper One said, waving her hand as she warmed up to the idea. "The point is, what are we going to do with the opportunity now that it's been presented to us?"

Piper Two's arms tickled with goose bumps. She smiled when Piper One looked down at her own arms, noting the same thing. They were *so* connected. This doubling thing had seemed creepy at first, but now she was starting to see all the useful aspects of it.

"I'll go to the interview and charm the pants off the reporter from the *Chronicle*," Piper Two offered.

"And I'll stay here and deal with the painters and any Darklighters that might show up,"

Piper One put in, smiling. "Then you can go to P3 and take care of Rinaldo while I bake!"

"Perfect!" Piper Two exclaimed.

They both stood up and started for the door that led to the foyer, but Piper One suddenly paused and grabbed Piper Two's arm. She immediately pulled her hand back. It was a little bizarre touching a person who was essentially herself. Now she knew what her body looked and felt like from the *outside* as well as the inside. This was way more intense than a mirror image. If she dwelled on it for too long, she knew it would freak her out.

"Wait a second," she said. "What about personal gain?"

"Hey. This is going to make us a much happier, saner witch," Piper Two told her, swinging her hair behind her shoulder. "It's for the greater good."

Piper One frowned thoughtfully and tilted her head. Normally she would have been the first to point out that that argument had never worked for them in the past, but right now she just didn't feel like it.

"Flimsy," she said with a grin that matched her double's. "But I'll take it."

Chapter 4

"You missed a spot on the ceiling there," Piper One said, pointing casually to the corner of the dining room where one of the painters was toiling away with his miniroller. He sighed loudly and slumped his shoulders. She'd been sitting at the table keeping a watchful eye on the workers ever since they had returned from their overly long break, and she could tell they were starting to tire of her. The problem for them was, she didn't remotely care.

"You gonna sit in here all day?" he asked, vigorously covering over the spot she'd indicated.

Smirking as she sorted through the paperwork they had destroyed that morning, Piper felt relaxed for the first time in days. "Yep," she told the man. "Is that a problem?" she added, folding her hands in her lap.

All three of the burly men, who were working

in separate areas of the room, exchanged fed-up looks. Piper ignored them and went happily back to sifting through her papers. They could complain about her as much as they wished. She wanted the job done right, and she was going to make sure these guys didn't slack off—now that she had the time.

But you only have the time because you worked a spell, a little voice prodded her. *A spell that is definitely in the realm of personal gain.*

Piper's heart gave an extra hard thump that she tried to ignore. If she dwelled too much on the fact that there was another Piper out there and what the consequences of that might be, then she knew she would never get anything done around here. And that was the whole point, wasn't it? Getting things done?

She would worry about the supernatural ramifications later. If and when they cropped up.

The phone rang and Piper picked up the cordless from the table in front of her and hit the talk button.

"Hello?"

"Piper? It's Piper," her own voice said from the other end of the line. It gave Piper One a chill to be talking to herself, but she smiled. This whole thing was also kind of cool.

"Hello there. How are things going?" Piper One asked Piper Two, leaning her elbows on the table and keeping one eye on the painters.

"I just got to the restaurant for the interview,

actually. I'm calling from my . . . our . . . cell," Piper Two replied. "Just wanted to check on the Darklighter situation. Any sightings?"

"None so far," Piper One said serenely, looking up at the ceiling as if she could see straight through to the attic. "I'll call you if anyone . . . pops in," she added, glancing around at the painters. She wasn't sure if it even mattered that she was speaking in code. They didn't seem like the brightest bunch anyway.

"Good. I'll keep the cell on me," Piper Two said.

"Oh! By the way, when you get to P3 later, there's this evil guy Douglas who works for Rinaldo," Piper One said quickly. She had to remember to fill Piper Two in on the missing chunks in her memory. They shared all memories up until the time Piper had left the house that morning, but after that, Piper Two had no way of knowing what Piper One had done. "Don't let him push you around."

"*Evil* evil or just evil?" Piper Two asked.

"Just evil," Piper One replied, then blinked, mulling it over. "I think. He wanted to break down all the walls in the VIP area to set up more seating for the fashion show."

"What? Is he *on* something?" Piper Two shrieked. "We can't destroy the VIP area!"

Do I really sound like that? Piper wondered, wincing. "Like I said, evil."

"Okay. I'm on it," Piper Two told her. "See you later!"

Piper One hung up the phone and sat back in her chair, feeling generally good about herself and her other self. It was so nice to be in such perfect symbiosis with someone—to know exactly what they were thinking and know that they understood you absolutely.

Yep. Piper could get used to this.

Piper Two tasted the wine the waiter had poured in her glass and smiled. Not too sweet, not too tart, a perfect wine for a business lunch. She waved her hand at him, indicating that she wanted him to pour full glasses for herself and Gina Manki, the impeccably dressed and coiffed reporter who was conducting the Businesswoman of the Year interview.

"You know your wine," Gina said with an impressed smile.

"Yes, well, I was in the restaurant business before I opened the club," Piper told her, shaking her hair back from her face and sipping her wine. Before leaving the Manor she had changed into a sleek, sleeveless black dress and added a bit more makeup to her eyes. It was more than she would have normally done on a Sunday afternoon, but she wanted to dress to impress and Gina seemed like the type of person who would notice—and had.

Piper smiled slightly as Gina tasted from her own glass. She couldn't believe how at ease she felt with this process. Usually she was not a person who enjoyed being put under the microscope. Talking about herself was not a favorite pastime.

"Right. That's in your bio," Gina said, checking a notebook she had laid in front of her. She held her pen between perfectly manicured fingers. "What made you switch from being a chef and restaurant manager to the nightclub biz?"

"Well, I wanted to run my own business and this club was available, so I guess it was meant to be," Piper said with a laugh.

"I'll say. You've turned quite a profit over the last few years," Gina commented. A lock of blond hair fell from her bun, and she quickly tucked it behind her ear.

"Well . . . give the people what they want . . . ," Piper said blithely, a casual smile playing about her lips.

Wow. I hardly even sound like myself, Piper thought, enjoying the confidence. *Who* is *this person?*

Gina laughed, making a note on her pad, and Piper knew she was nailing this interview. She took a deep breath and let it out slowly, letting the feeling of giddy euphoria wash over her. There was no way she could have done this if she didn't know her double was at home right now, dealing with everything else. Not only that, but dealing with everything else in the exact way *she* would deal with it. Phoebe and Paige were responsible and she trusted their opinions, but Piper had always been a person who liked things done a particular way—she was a lot more comfortable with her own instincts. Had she not made that wish, she'd be distracted right now—itching to pick up her cell and check on things—but as it was, she was free to be as charming as humanly possible.

"Your lunch, ladies," the waiter said, placing plates of stylishly arranged food in front of them.

"It looks wonderful, thank you," Piper said, lifting her fork. The food smelled delicious—and the whole meal was being paid for by the *San Francisco Chronicle*. Suddenly Piper was congratulating herself not only for conjuring up a double, but for choosing to take the out-of-house responsibilities. Lunching with Gina at a gourmet restaurant was a lot more fun than sitting home at the Manor surrounded by those odoriferous painters and waiting to blow up any Darklighters that might dare to show their ugly faces.

It was good to be Piper Two.

Piper hummed along to the radio as she mixed the ingredients for her famous chocolate-raspberry cupcakes, even swaying her hips slightly to the beat. The painters had cleared out for the day, and she had the kitchen all to herself. The sun was starting to lower in the sky and a cool breeze ruffled the curtains, whisking away the paint-scented air and replacing it with the fresh scent of spring rain.

This could very well be the greatest night of my life, Piper thought as she spooned the mixture into the cupcake tins. She knew she was exaggerating, but at that moment it didn't feel that way. It had been a long time since she'd been able to take her time and enjoy cooking or baking. Lately everything she made was done in a rush with ten other things on her mind. It seemed she'd forgotten how much fun it could be. That it wasn't just a responsibility, but an enjoyable process—and something she was really *good* at.

Piper popped the first batch of cupcakes into the oven and set the timer with a little flourish of her hand, laughing out loud at her own silliness. It was okay. Paige and Phoebe had been holed up in the attic for hours, so they weren't around to witness it. She executed a little spin move to the music, grabbing up a new mixing bowl to get to work on the batter for the walnut muffins—Leo's favorite.

Leo, Piper thought. It would be so nice to see him right now. She was in such a good mood and she would like nothing better than to share it with him. Piper placed the bowl down on the counter and looked up. Might as well give it a shot.

"Leo!" she called, her mouth working into a crooked smile. "Oh, Leeeooo!"

Piper waited, blinking at the ceiling, but nothing happened. No swirl of lights, no nothing. He must be *really* busy.

Oh well, Piper thought, pulling all the ingredients together. *Maybe I'll try again when the muffins are done and they're all nice and warm.* She could just picture the appreciative look on his face when he bit into one of them. She giggled just thinking about it.

I hope the other me is having as much fun as I am, Piper thought, sifting the flour. Unfortunately, since Piper Two was probably dealing with Douglas right about now, that just didn't seem possible.

Piper stood back as the workers carted everything out of the VIP areas, making sure they kept each alcove's pillows, curtains, and cushions separate so that they could go back where they came from when the new floor was finished. Pounding and sawing filled the air, and the acrid yet clean scent of cut wood tickled her nostrils. The place was bustling. She liked it.

Her cell phone rang, and Piper's heart shot up toward her mouth. She turned and grabbed it from the bar, not surprised to see the Manor's number displayed on the caller ID screen. She hit the talk button and brought the phone to her ear.

"Hello?" she said, tucking her hair furtively behind her ear. "Everything okay?"

"Everything's fiiiine," her own voice trilled lazily back at her. "Just wanted to check in on you."

"Jeez. You scared me half to death," Piper Two replied. "I thought something happened to Paige."

"Sorry," Piper One said. "I guess I should have realized you'd react that way. I mean, since I probably would have."

"Exactly," Piper Two replied with a sigh.

"All right, Ms. Halliwell, I have your flooring options."

A man who had to be the Douglas guy Piper One had warned her about walked up with a couple of samples. Piper half-smiled the moment she saw him, taking in his sleek suit and chiseled chin. What Piper One hadn't warned her about was the fact that he was take-your-breath-away handsome.

"I'll be right there," she said, lifting one finger. She turned away from him and whispered into the phone. "Why didn't you tell me this Douglas guy was so hot?"

"What? Ew," Piper One said. "He's so not our type."

"Yeah, yeah, yeah," Piper Two said. "Well, everything's fine here. Nothing to worry about. See you later, 'bye!"

She hung up the phone quickly, knowing Piper One was probably standing in the kitchen staring in shock at the phone, and returned her attention to Douglas. Wow, his eyes were piercing.

"Well, let's take a look," Piper said, leading him over to the deserted bar. Luckily P3 was closed on Sunday nights, so the crew was free to work until the wee hours of the morning and into tomorrow. Piper was starting to think this fashion show was the best idea she'd ever had. It was forcing her to give the club a long-overdue renovation.

"These are the two they can put in before tomorrow night," Douglas said flatly, laying the two samples, both black and shiny, on the bar. "This one is more durable and clearly the better choice, but it's also more expensive, so I assume *you'll* be going with the other."

"What makes you think that?" Piper asked with a flash of irritation.

Douglas blinked at her, his expression condescending. "Well, you seem resistant to everything else I say. Plus, it's clear to me that you enjoy cutting corners," he added with a slight sneer.

Piper narrowed her eyes slightly. Where did this guy get off? She was starting to understand Piper One's warning that he was evil.

"Look, my VIP areas are important to me *and* to my regular patrons, so no, I didn't want to spend tons of money so that you could knock the walls down and destroy them," Piper said, picking up the more expensive sample. "But if this is the better floor, then this is the floor I want."

For the first time Douglas's eyes softened and he almost looked impressed. "Good," he said, pulling a pen out of his breast pocket and clicking the button at the top. He made a note in his leather binder, then pulled out his cell phone. "I'll put the order in right now."

"Great," Piper said, pushing away from the bar. She figured that since she actually had some extra time on her hands for once, she might get started on this month's inventory. It had been a long time since she'd been able to get a head start on anything.

Douglas turned away and started to dial a number on his cell, but then reconsidered and faced her again. "You know, you're a lot easier to work with tonight than you were this morning."

Piper smiled. "Well, let's just say I've got a lot less on my shoulders tonight," she said. *Like about half of what I had this morning,* she added silently.

"I like the change," Douglas told her, eyeing her appreciatively. Piper almost blushed under his gaze. The guy was flirting with her! She couldn't remember the last time she'd been flirted with. Not that she'd ever cheat on Leo, but still, it was nice. Even if the guy could be kind of a jerk.

"Would you like to have dinner with me tonight?" Douglas asked.

"I don't think that's such a good idea," Piper replied, lifting her hand to show him her wedding ring.

"A business dinner," Douglas said smoothly,

barely acknowledging the ring with a flick of his eyes. "We have a lot to discuss."

Piper had a feeling that Douglas was interested in more than business, but she wasn't, so where was the harm? Besides, Douglas's obvious admiration made her feel attractive, sexy, and confident—and she liked the sensation. It was very different from the old-married-woman aura she'd been functioning in lately.

It's not cheating. It's just dinner, she told herself.

"Okay," she told him. "A business dinner."

"Great," Douglas responded, flashing his pearly whites. "I'll just make this call and we'll go."

Piper turned away from him under the pretense of gathering her things, and hid her giddy smile. Her sisters would be so proud of her. It was time to have a little more of that fun thing.

Chapter 5

"How long have we been up here?" Paige asked, stretching her arms and letting out a huge yawn.

Phoebe worked the kinks out of her neck and sniffed the air. "Muffins! Piper must be baking. Time for a chocolate break," she said.

Somehow just moving away from the podium where the Book sat gave her a head rush. She checked her watch and realized she hadn't moved in over an hour. Her stomach grumbled angrily. Paige was holding a hand over her own abdomen as if she'd just experienced the same thing. They were working themselves into the ground here, and so far they had found exactly one page on wishes and wish reversal. All it said was that for a wish to come true, the person had to put his or her entire heart into the wish. The same was true to reverse it.

It all sounded like fairy-tale mumbo jumbo to Phoebe.

"I hope Piper made some fresh coffee, too," Paige said. "I'll stay here and keep looking. Just bring me back some provisions—I could use a little pick-me-up."

"Definitely," Phoebe answered.

As she descended the stairs from the attic, her head felt thick, her eyes tired and dry. Phoebe hated to admit it, but she was feeling rather hopeless. As difficult as it was to accept, admit, and comprehend, Phoebe was starting to think that unless someone had an epiphany soon, the Power of Three was going to be the Power of Four—for good.

As if this house isn't already crowded enough, Phoebe thought.

It was kind of ironic, actually, that it had been Piper of all people who had messed up in a way that brought her such obvious personal gain. Except for a couple of infractions here and there, Piper had always been the cautious one—the one who lectured Phoebe and Paige endlessly on the drawbacks and potential dangers of personal gain. If anyone came close to breaking the rules, Piper was there to stop them.

And now she has a double, Phoebe thought, smiling slightly. *What I wouldn't give for another one of me. I could help two times more people with my column, or send one of me out to deal with work while the other me got a facial. . . .*

Phoebe laughed at her daydream and was about to shuffle into the kitchen for a snack when she noticed that Piper—one of the Pipers, anyway—was sacked out on the couch watching TV. She had her arm crooked behind her head and her legs crossed at the ankle and seemed totally relaxed. Like there wasn't another one of her walking around somewhere, messing up the cosmic scheme of things.

Both Phoebe and Paige had been wondering where the Pipers were for the last couple of hours, but had decided that the new twins were probably dealing with the strangeness of their situation and maybe even coming up with their own solution. Paige had suggested they leave the Pipers alone for a while and Phoebe had agreed, but she felt a little rush of irritation at seeing one of them lazing around.

"Hey," Phoebe said, arching her back to stretch some coiled muscles as she walked into the room. She reached her arms above her head and yawned. "I thought you guys were going to come upstairs and help us."

"I figured you two had it covered," Piper replied. "I hung out and kept an eye on the painters until they left and then started the baking."

"Oh. Well, that's . . . good, I guess," Phoebe said, trying to keep her irritation at bay. It wasn't easy, however. Hadn't she and Paige just spent hours trying to figure out how to clean up *Piper's* magical mess? "Where's Piper Two?"

"How did you know I was Piper One?" Piper asked, glancing up for half a second.

"I don't think that girl is ever going to take off that jacket of hers," Phoebe replied matter-of-factly.

Piper smiled slightly and picked up a piece of popcorn from a bowl on the floor. Unbelievable. While Phoebe and Paige were going cross-eyed staring at the Book of Shadows, Piper was chilling with the painters, baking, and now chowing down and watching a repeat of some reality show.

Bite your tongue, Phoebe told herself. It was good that Piper could kick back under the circumstances . . . kind of.

"She went to P3," Piper said, munching away. "We decided it would be good to get a few things done while we could."

"Piper—"

"I know! I know! I'm vegging right now," Piper said. "But do you know how long it's been since I've had time to watch TV? I've been wondering what this whole reality trend that everyone's talking about is," she joked.

"That's . . . great," Phoebe said slowly. "But do you really think it's a good idea that there's another you out there doing who knows what?"

"What's she going to do?" Piper asked, her brow furrowing. "I mean, she's me, right? She won't do anything I wouldn't do."

Phoebe began to process this, then shook her head. Hours of Book-of-Shadows studying had strained her brain, and the whole "She's me, I'm her" concept was a little too much for her at the moment. She decided to move on to her next concern rather than dwell.

"Okay, but aren't you at all worried about personal gain?" Phoebe asked, appealing to Piper's normally overactive conscience. Phoebe sat down next to her sister's legs on the couch and blocked her view of the television. This felt like a full-attention-required kind of conversation—and Piper had only ripped her eyes from the screen once since they'd started talking.

Now Piper sat up slightly, pushing her hands into the cushion at her sides. "A little," she admitted, though not too convincingly. "But Piper Two made a good point earlier. I was overworked and hassled and I did need help. Maybe this all happened for a reason."

"Piper—"

"No, I'm serious, Phoebe," Piper said. "This way my brain won't be all over the place, and it'll be easier for me to focus on things—including supernatural things."

Like you've been doing today? Phoebe thought, but opted to keep her mouth shut. The last thing they needed was to have an argument.

"Having Piper Two around will make me . . . us . . . whatever, better witches, which in turn will help innocents, which can't really be construed as personal gain," Piper finished.

Yeah. Nice try, Phoebe thought.

"You sound like me when I used to try to talk

myself out of getting grounded," she said.

"Should I take that as a compliment?" Piper asked hopefully.

"I'm not so sure," Phoebe replied, slumping back over Piper's legs and leaning into the couch.

She sighed and stared down at the floor, realizing she was relieved on some level to have just one Piper in the house. It was simply too weird to have two of them in the same room. Phoebe couldn't seem to figure out who she was talking to and was somehow always surprised when both of them responded. And Piper was right, Piper Two was still Piper. It wasn't like they had to worry about her running around, blowing things up for sport or telling everyone about their witchy powers.

Still, Phoebe wanted to solve this. She *needed* to solve this. Piper may have been enjoying her doubled efficiency, but it just wasn't natural.

"I wish Leo were here," Phoebe said quietly, gazing up at the ceiling.

"He'll come as soon as he's done Up There," Piper said, patting Phoebe's knee in a reassuring yet dismissive kind of way. "Don't worry."

"Yeah, but we still don't know what this whole Darklighter thing is about," Phoebe said, training her ear toward the ceiling to make sure that Paige was still peacefully studying the Book. There were no sounds of attack or struggle. "The more time that passes without something happening, the more on edge I get."

"What, you *want* a Darklighter to show up?" Piper asked.

"No! I just want to know what they're planning—and Leo's the only one who might know anything," Phoebe said, rubbing at her forehead. She wanted at least *one* thing to be resolved—either the Piper mess or the Darklighter threat—but she was no closer to solving either problem.

"I'm sure it's fine. Like you said, if the Darklighter was after Paige, he would have tried to kill her when he had the chance," Piper said, leaning back again and refocusing her eyes on the TV. "The Elders must've gotten their wires crossed somehow."

"I hope you're right," Phoebe replied. She glanced at her sister, but Piper's eyes were glued to the screen yet again.

Clearly Piper wanted to get back to her all-important TV watching, so Phoebe pushed herself up from the couch and headed for the kitchen and some fresh-baked muffins.

"I'm sure it's fine." Right, she thought sarcastically. Phoebe had a bad feeling about all of this, and sometimes a pep talk from Leo was the only thing that could make her feel better—it was one of his patented Whitelighter talents. Plus, if she could just tell him what was going on with Piper, he might be able to talk to the Elders about a solution.

I just hope his higher-power meetings end soon,

Phoebe thought, pouring coffee. *If there was ever a time I could use a little Whitelighter guidance, it's now.*

From the kitchen, Phoebe heard Piper laugh at the TV, and she paused.

In order for a wish to come true, the person has to put his or her entire heart into the wish. The same is true to reverse it.

Was it possible? Could it be that Piper One and Piper Two were so happy with this new arrangement that they didn't want in their hearts to be one again? If so, it would explain why the reverse wish hadn't worked.

Phoebe shook her head and scoffed at herself. No. No way. This was Piper she was talking about. Her heart, or *hearts,* had to have been in that wish. If there was one thing Phoebe knew about Piper, it was that she liked things orderly—and there was no way her sister would think it was cosmically correct for there to be two of her walking the Earth. She was way too smart for that.

Piper Two sat back in the passenger seat of Douglas's black, retro Thunderbird convertible, the wind in her hair, a sophisticated jazz tune pumping from the speakers, and thought that considering the way this day had started out, it hadn't ended up so badly. The sky was clear, the stars were out, the air was warm. Douglas had sprung for a killer five-course meal at a restaurant normal people had to wait months to get in to and the wait staff had treated them like gods. Now they were zipping through the streets of San Francisco, driving just a tad too fast, catching admiring glances everywhere they went. People couldn't seem to take their eyes off Douglas and Piper.

And why not? Piper thought. *We're a beautiful couple in a hot car. Well, not a* couple, *but they don't know that.*

"I have a little surprise," Douglas said, screeching the car around a corner and heading onto a dark street. The guy drove like Jeff Gordon, but was somehow totally at ease and nonchalant about it. Piper was amazed. She broke a sweat if she went more than five miles an hour above the speed limit.

"Surprises are good," Piper said.

Sometimes, she added silently.

Piper looked at her surroundings, noticing the sudden lack of overhead lights. Her Charmed One senses went on alert. More bad things had happened to her in dark alleyways and on back streets than she cared to recall. She was just starting to grow paranoid that Douglas was taking her to an uninhabited part of the city for a sinister reason, when she saw the outline of a huge crowd of people jamming the sidewalk up ahead.

"What's going on?" Piper asked.

"This is that new club, Bubble," Douglas told her, downshifting and pulling up at the curb. A few dozen heads turned to take in the new arrival. "Rinaldo is entertaining some friends here tonight."

"Wait a minute, Rinaldo is hanging out at my competition?" Piper asked as a valet came over and popped open her door. Piper sat back and crossed her arms over her chest. "I'm not going in there."

"Don't be a child, Piper," Douglas said, stepping out of the car and tossing the keys to the valet. "You need to go in there. Don't you want to keep an eye on your competitors?"

The man did have a point. Piper sighed, eyeing the crowd. She had to admit that inside she was dying of curiosity. There had to be a hundred people there, some of the "beautiful people" of San Francisco, and each more stylishly dressed than the next. What would bring in such a throng on a Sunday night?

Maybe I should start rethinking that whole closing on Sundays thing, Piper thought.

As she watched, a group of ten girls and two guys approached a huge bouncer. He unhooked the rope, letting most of the girls pass, but stretching out his beefy arm before the guys and the last two women could get through. Piper noted that these women weren't quite as attractive as those who had been allowed in. A bunch of people still waiting in line laughed as the unfortunates turned and skulked away. Piper hated when clubs discriminated like that—she would never turn people away based on looks or the way they dressed—but it did make her wonder what the crowd inside looked like.

"All right," she said finally, placing one foot on the ground. "I'm not exactly dressed for it, though." She was still wearing the expensive, yet conservative black dress she'd donned for her interview with Gina that afternoon, along with a pair of not-so-high heels. The only thing she had that was even remotely cool was her new leather jacket.

"Doesn't matter. They'll let you in," Douglas said, offering his arm. She half expected him to comment on her beauty and how it would bewitch the bouncers, but she had given him too much credit. "You're with me and I'm on the guest list," he told her cockily.

Piper checked her cell phone quickly to make sure no one had tried to call. She was surprised—in a good way, of course—that there had been no emergencies, considering everything that had gone on earlier that afternoon. But then again, if anything *had* happened, there was another Piper there to deal with it. They didn't even have to bother calling her. Piper wasn't sure if she felt happy about that, or slightly sad. As the big sister, it was disconcerting not to be needed. But Douglas was tugging on her elbow, so she shoved her cell phone back in her bag, deciding to think about it later.

Piper and Douglas breezed by the clamoring

crowd and the bouncer gave them the once-over before checking his list. Piper flushed slightly under his gaze, knowing he must have been wondering what the PTA mom was doing out so late on a Sunday. Douglas merely held his chin a bit higher and waited until the oversized man grunted and stepped aside to let them pass. All the people behind them groaned and pressed a bit closer to the door when the pair was let in. Piper had to admit it made her feel kind of cool to be one of the chosen—even if they had kind of cheated by being on the list.

Once inside, it was blatantly clear why the club was called Bubble. There were shimmering bubbles everywhere—shooting out of the walls, up from vents in the floor, cascading down from the ceiling. The owner must have spent a veritable fortune on bubble machines, not to mention gallons of bubble formula. As Douglas pulled Piper through the gleeful, gyrating crowd on the round, rotating dance floor, bubbles popped against her face and hands, tickling her skin and actually prompting a few giggles. It was a pleasant, almost uplifting sensation.

Multicolored discs decorated the black walls and hung from the ceiling on invisible strings. A waitress on roller skates slid by, deftly balancing a silver tray of bubbling blue soda bottles, each sporting a different-colored straw. Piper could have sworn her dress was made out of bubble wrap.

All the chairs and couches along the walls were round-backed and had round seats. They sat on rugs that were woven with brightly colored circles. The circular bar itself was made of glass and had hundreds of tiny bubbles dancing through the clear liquid underneath the surface. Passing by, Piper could have sworn she saw a few of her regulars from P3 chilling and helping themselves to handfuls of the free bubble gum that sat in jars all along the counter.

Traitors, Piper thought. But she had a hard time stoking the fires of her indignation. If she were perfectly honest with herself, she could see why so many people were dying to get in here. The place was rocking.

Paige and Phoebe would love this scene, Piper thought, smiling slightly and wondering if she should call them and see if they wanted to stop by. But she pushed the idea aside. Her sisters were dealing with more important things at the moment. Things that Piper Two didn't much want to think about. Not when everyone around her seemed to be having so much carefree fun.

Douglas dove through a curtain made of thousands of clear, hanging beads, and Piper saw Rinaldo holding court at the far end of a small, round room. He was surrounded by models, photographers, and Rinaldo wanna-bes. There were at least three men in the room with shaved heads, berets, and totally overdone outfits. A strung-out looking girl in the corner blew bubbles from a wand into the air, then tried to catch them on her tongue.

"Piper! Douglas! You made it!" Rinaldo trilled when he saw the couple walk in. He air-kissed Piper and gripped her shoulders, staring at her meaningfully. "Trust me when I tell you I only came here because your club wasn't open. This place doesn't hold a candle to P3. Or a bubble," he added with a horselike laugh, touching her shoulder companionably.

How clever, Piper thought.

"I have to disagree," she said diplomatically as she scanned the room. "I think it's great."

"So humble," Rinaldo said, looking at the ceiling with a proud-papa sort of expression that gave Piper a bit of the creeps. After all, she'd just met the guy. She wasn't even sure if Rinaldo was his first or last name. Didn't any of these people find the intimacy they forced upon each other to be kind of . . . off-putting?

"I love this girl!" Rinaldo announced to the room, pulling Piper into him. Everyone around them cheered and lifted their glasses. Piper, at first totally uncomfortable being held against Rinaldo's side, soon found herself grinning uncontrollably even as she held her breath. Okay, so maybe a bit of blind admiration wasn't *all* bad. It could never take the place of true love and deep emotion, of course, but when was the last time random people had cheered for her or eyed her with such blatant envy and admiration? Only

Douglas's smile seemed to convey a sort of sarcasm—an understanding of the fact that all the emotions flowing through the small room were more shallow than most puddles.

Piper knew this was true, but decided to enjoy it anyway.

"Don't you love this girl?" Rinaldo shouted, causing another round of cheers. "To Piper!" he added, thrusting his champagne glass in the air.

"To Piper!" A couple of dozen people she'd never met shouted, clinking glasses and tossing back their drinks.

Someone pressed a fresh flute of bubbly into her hand and the foam overflowed onto the floor. Piper raised her drink modestly, playing along, then took a sip. The champagne was fabulous—light and sweet—and Piper's expert taste buds told her that Rinaldo and his friends were swilling the good stuff. Probably hundreds of dollars per bottle. She gulped down a bit more and her glass was quickly refilled.

"To Piper!" a girl's very slurred voice shouted again and another toast went up. Piper grinned. The whole thing might have been silly, but she didn't want to be a spoilsport. Besides, how could she not get the least bit caught up in the atmosphere? If Rinaldo loved her, it seemed everyone else loved her. And it wasn't every day the beautiful people applauded her very existence.

"Come on." A gorgeous blond woman of

Amazonian proportions grabbed Piper by the arm and pulled her out of Rinaldo's grasp. She was wearing so much eyeliner she looked as if she'd come straight from a bar brawl—that she'd lost. "Come dance with us."

Piper struggled to find an empty bit of table on which to place her glass. "I don't think—"

"Oh, come on! The night is young!" another model insisted. This girl was showing more leg than Piper even *had*. Her skin seemed to glisten in the flashing strobe lights. "Let's go, Piper! Live a little!"

Piper shook off the odd sensation of a complete stranger calling her by name. She had to appreciate their enthusiasm. Laughing at their continued cajoling, she finally allowed herself to be dragged out to the dance floor by the two women who towered over her. She cast a help-me look at Douglas who shrugged and smiled his smirky smile as she disappeared through the hanging beads. Piper wasn't at all surprised. It wasn't as if she actually expected the guy to come to her aid. He wasn't, after all, her man.

And thank God for that, a little voice in her mind said.

Still, she had to be grateful to Douglas. If not for him, she never would have come here. And she liked it here. A lot.

Out in the club the music was pumping, the crowd was exploding with energy, and Piper was soon sucked into the vibe. It took a few minutes to get her bearings on the ever-moving dance floor, but once she did, she couldn't stop dancing. It was such an intense release. Any residual tension from the early stress of her day was soon washed away on the pulsating beat.

When Rinaldo came out to join the girls, the crowd formed a reverent circle around the A-listers and Piper found herself dancing in front of a throng of onlookers, but somehow she didn't even care. Bubbles were popping, her hair was starting to grow sticky, and all she could do was laugh. Who knew clubbing could be so much fun? She'd been running a club for so long, she'd forgotten how it felt to just be a patron. It was so freeing to not have to worry about the music, the wait staff, or if there was enough ice.

It's starting to get late, a little voice in her mind warned. *You should go home and find out if Phoebe and Paige have come up with a solution.*

But that could wait, couldn't it? She was having so much fun. And besides, there was another Piper at home to deal with the supernatural stuff. And that Piper had her sisters to help her. It was a combination that had always worked in the past, so why mess with it?

That other Piper can be the responsible one, Piper thought, feeling naughty and liking it. Unlike earlier, Piper was now certain that the fact her family didn't need her was a *good* thing. Let someone else do the worrying for a change. She pulled away from the dancing long enough to make one guilty phone call home—the girls had no news for her, but Piper figured she'd done her duty.

For this Piper, it was time to party.

Chapter 6

"Any luck?" Piper One asked, strolling into the attic to find her sisters sitting next to each other on the couch, the Book of Shadows open over both their laps. Pieces of crumpled paper surrounded them on the cushions and the floor, and Phoebe had her bottom lip squeezed between her forefinger and thumb as she bent to study the spell before her. Paige tapped a pen against the side of the book maniacally, then paused to take a long sip from her favorite mug.

"Not exactly," Phoebe said, flipping the page. "I found that spell that Prue used to triple herself a couple years back, but that doesn't help us since her clones were supposed to disappear once their mission was fulfilled." Phoebe looked up from the Book. "You and your double don't have a mission."

"Unless our mission is to make my life easier,

which we already have," Piper said lightly. She sat down across from Paige and Phoebe and crossed her legs at the knee. Her sisters exchanged a disturbed, knowing look that Piper chose to ignore. "I mean, don't you think the wish might have worked for a reason? Maybe the cosmos sensed I needed a little help."

"I don't think so, Piper," Paige said. Her expression was apologetic. "We all get stressed out once in a while, but the cosmos doesn't usually send us a double to help take the load off."

"I know. But it *is* kind of nice," Piper said.

Phoebe and Paige exchanged a look. "Piper, we have to ask you something," Paige said tentatively.

"What?" Piper asked.

"When you and Piper Two wished to be one again . . . did you really want for it to happen?" Paige asked.

"Of course I did!" Piper replied. "Paige, how could you even ask me that?"

"It was just a theory," Phoebe told her. "We found something that says your whole heart has to be in a wish for it to work."

"And since you seem so . . . *happy* to have a double—," Paige put in.

"You guys, come on. I'm saying it's convenient," Piper said. "But the second we find a way to fix it, I'm in. Trust me."

Both Phoebe and Paige looked relieved. Piper

felt offended that they'd doubted her. Didn't her sisters know her at all?

Piper took a deep breath and sighed. Why couldn't they just let her enjoy the freedom while she had it? Being a Charmed One had taken a lot of things away from Piper over the years. It had given her a lot too, granted—like Leo and Paige and the satisfaction of helping people and ridding the world of certain evils. But all of that had been at the expense of so many other things—other family members' lives, for one thing. But also friends, a life, knowing that she was safe instead of constantly wondering when the next demon would attack. Piper Two seemed like a gift to her. Payback for everything she went through on a daily basis. And she deserved it, however temporary it might turn out to be.

Phoebe opened her mouth to say something, but the phone rang and Piper jumped up, saved by the bell. "I'll get it!"

She jogged downstairs, happy to be away from the heavy, negative vibe in the attic. The last thing she wanted to hear were more reasons this whole thing was wrong. She headed into her room and grabbed the phone.

"Hello?" she said, slightly out of breath.

"Yes, may I speak to Piper Halliwell, please?" a polite female voice asked.

"This is she," Piper said. *One of she, anyway,* she added silently, smirking.

"Piper, this is Gina from the *San Francisco Chronicle*?" the woman said. "I just wanted to thank you again for meeting with me this afternoon."

Piper's heart skipped a beat. *She* hadn't met with this woman. Piper Two had. What if she referenced something Piper Two had said over lunch and Piper had no idea what she was talking about?

"Are you there?" Gina asked. "Damn cell phone," she said under her breath.

"No! I'm here!" Piper said, pacing a bit. She held the phone to her ear with both hands as if it was going to keep her from missing something. "I . . . well, you're welcome. It was . . . fun." *I think,* she added silently. *Please let lunch have been fun.*

"I know! I had such a great time," Gina told her, causing Piper to sigh with relief. "And just between you and me, I don't think you'll have any trouble picking up that award."

"Really?" Piper blurted before she could check herself. She brought her hand to her head. *Oh. Very sophisticated,* she thought. "I mean, that's great news."

"Well, I know *my* recommendation is going to be glowing," Gina assured her. "Maybe we can do it again sometime. I'd love to just hang out. I told my friends about some of the lesser-known restaurants you recommended and they're dying to try them."

Oh God. Which restaurants? Piper wondered.

But then she immediately knew that Piper Two had probably mentioned Bania's, The Frog and the Peach, and the Takima Steakhouse—Piper's three little-known favorites.

She is me, after all, Piper reminded herself.

"Absolutely," she said. "Bania's has a special menu on Fridays—only the chef's favorites. Maybe we can all go next week."

"Don't you have that big fashion show to get ready for on Saturday night?" Gina asked.

"Oh, I can probably swing both," Piper said with a smile.

"That's so great! I'll call you later in the week to make plans!" Gina trilled.

"Perfect," Piper said, trying not to dwell on the fact that this woman was acting like they were old friends and she'd never even laid eyes on her. Piper Two must have been seriously impressive to merit not only stellar praise, but the offer of a friendship as well.

Suddenly Piper felt a warmth start to spread through her chest. Gina seemed so nice. Plus she had said that Piper could really win the Businesswoman of the Year Award. How amazing would it be to be recognized for all her hard work at P3? And all thanks to Piper Two!

She so loved having a double.

"Well, thanks again, Piper," Gina said. "I'll be in touch."

"Great. Thank *you*!" Piper said before hanging up.

"Yes!" Piper said under her breath, grinning as a bubble of pride welled up within her. She started upstairs again but paused halfway to the attic. This news was worth sharing with her sisters, but somehow, she didn't want to go back up into that room. She had a feeling that Paige and Phoebe would have a hard time mustering up the proper level of excitement in their current moods. They were so tired and stressed and worried, and those were three things Piper didn't want to be right now. She wanted to be happy for herself.

Thinking she'd rejoin Phoebe and Paige in a little while, Piper went back to her bedroom and called for Leo. Maybe he'd be between meetings and could orb down to celebrate with her for a few minutes. She waited a few seconds after saying his name, but Leo didn't come.

"Leo!" Piper whisper-shouted, looking up at the ceiling. "Come on, Leo. Give me a break here!"

But there was no response. Piper's heart skipped with a slight case of fear, but she pushed it aside. Leo had warned them about this, after all. There was nothing to be concerned about. There would be plenty of time to tell him about the day's successes later.

There was a book sitting on her nightstand that Piper had been wanting to read forever. She grabbed it and wiped the dust from the cover, then settled in on the bed, propping the pillows behind her. She would read a chapter or so and then either go back up to the attic or try Leo again. He had to hear her eventually.

She couldn't concentrate on her reading, though. Laying the book aside, Piper tried one last time.

"Leo! I'm alone in the *bedroom*!" she sing-songed. Again, nothing. Piper rolled her eyes, slumped back, and cracked open her book. Whatever those meetings were about up there, they must have been *really* important.

Leo stood with a few of his Whitelighter friends among the white, puffy clouds outside the Great Room, on break from the seemingly endless stream of meetings. All around them, other Whitelighters spoke to one another softly, stretched their limbs, and walked to loosen themselves up. The meetings were running longer than any of them would have predicted, and even though they were the most patient beings in the universe, the Whitelighters were growing restless.

Some more restless than others, Leo thought, wishing his heart would stop the hammering beat it had taken up ever since Mariah's announcement about the Darklighters. Whenever the Whitelighters were inside the Great Room, calls from their charges were blocked, which meant that if the girls had been trying to contact him, he wouldn't have been able to hear them. If something *had* gone wrong, his only hope was for one of them to call him now, while he was on a break, and then he would be allowed to go to them. In the meantime, all he could do was hope for news from Lauren and the Elders.

Glancing around, Leo tried to spot one of the Elders, but they all seemed to have gone off somewhere together—there wasn't a single one in sight. Leo wasn't sure whether this was a bad sign, or whether they were just talking among themselves about the proceedings. He needed to find out if Lauren had gotten the message about the Darklighters to Paige and if they had learned anything else.

The suspense was killing him. He needed to know everything was all right.

"All this just to decide whether or not to add another Elder post," Leo's old friend and colleague Barnabus said with a yawn. "Why do they have to make everything so complicated?"

Shana, another, more senior Whitelighter, smiled placatingly. "There are rules to be followed. Procedures to adhere to. These procedures have worked for thousands of years," she said. "You shouldn't question their ways."

"I don't know. I think Barnabus is right," Leo put in, trying to focus on the conversation at hand. "Maybe we should take another look at the system. It doesn't have to be so involved."

"Why am I not surprised that the rule-breaker wants to break the rules?" Shana joked, raising her eyebrows.

Leo flushed slightly and looked at the swirling white ground beneath him. The other Whitelighters were always teasing him for marrying Piper—for putting himself through all the drama and heartache he went through to be with her. But it had all been worth it. Not only did he get to be with the woman of his dreams, but their marriage had changed the rules forever. Because of Leo and Piper, and the success of their marriage, other Whitelighters might not have such a hard time in the future, were they to fall in love with mortals or witches.

"I'm not talking about breaking the rules, I'm talking about reassessing them," Leo said with a small smile, taking a moment to scan the crowd for the Elders once again. There was something amiss—he could sense it. At this point he would have been glad just for a glimpse of Lauren's blond hair, but he hadn't seen any of the Whitelighter novices since the meeting had adjourned. "Sometimes change is a good thing," he added.

"Yeah. After all, it got you a wife," Barnabus joked, tapping Leo's shoulder with the back of his hand.

"Leo!"

Piper, Leo thought, hearing her voice in his mind. His heart still skipped a few beats whenever she summoned him. It was a nice feeling, even after all this time. Plus she didn't sound distressed, which meant that Paige was probably fine. Relief washed over Leo like a warm blanket, and he smiled.

"What is it?" Barnabus asked.

"Gotta go," Leo replied, shrugging apologetically at his friends. He pulled off his robe, figuring he might as well go down and check on things. Piper may not have sounded upset, but she must have been calling him for a reason.

"Who's calling?" Shana asked, a knowing smile playing about her full lips.

"It's Piper," he confirmed with a grin. "I'll be right back."

"When duty calls," Barnabus said good-naturedly, taking Leo's robe from him.

Leo was just about to orb out when a disturbance off to his left caught his attention. The Whitelighters were all scurrying out of the way to let a group of Elders pass. They were coming on quickly, heading straight for Leo and his friends. A lump of dread formed in Leo's throat. He didn't even care that the Elders were about to catch him in his civilian clothes. Clearly there were more important things at hand.

"Leo," Shia said, his expression grave. "We need to speak with you."

"What is it?" Leo asked, following the Elders off to a more deserted area. Barnabus and Shana exchanged a concerned glance, but knew enough not to follow unless they were summoned. Piper called to Leo again, and it pained him to have to ignore her.

"It's Lauren," Mariah said, stepping to the foreground. "She never returned from her mission."

Leo felt all the blood rush from his face. "What? What happened?" he demanded.

"We believe a Darklighter might have gotten to her before she was able to deliver her message," Shia explained.

"They must be watching the Manor. That's it. I'm going down there right now," Leo said resolutely.

"Yes, do that," Mariah told him. "But make sure you come back here quickly and bring Paige with you. We now believe your hunch was right. The Darklighters must be planning some kind of action against the Charmed Ones. We need to keep her safe until this danger has passed."

Should've listened to me the first time, Leo thought, but he kept his mouth shut. This was no time for petty arguments. He nodded at the Elders and orbed out, picturing his and Piper's bedroom at the Manor in his mind. All he could think about was getting to his family and protecting them.

The second Leo orbed, however, he knew something was wrong. Normally it took a split second for him to reappear wherever he wanted to go, but in his in-between state, he suddenly felt as if something had grabbed hold of him—as if he were caught in a huge net. Leo tried to reconstitute himself—to regain his tangible form—but he couldn't. As much as he strained against the pliable substance that seemed to bind him, he couldn't break free.

What the hell is going on? Leo thought, starting to panic. *What* is *this?*

In all his years as a Whitelighter, nothing like this had ever happened to him. He felt as if he couldn't breathe. Suddenly he was jerked backward and felt as if he was being sucked through the ether. He was speeding through space, whirling and tumbling and unable to control himself.

Piper! Piper, help! Leo called out desperately, knowing it wouldn't do any good. He had no voice—only his thoughts—and she would never have been able to hear him anyway. Alone, scared, and thinking only of Paige's safety, Leo flew faster and faster, growing more and more disoriented as he spun and spun and spun—until finally, mercifully, he blacked out.

With the book open in her lap and her back pressed into the pillows on her bed, Piper felt her eyes start to grow heavy. They blinked closed a few times and she shook her head, struggling to stay awake. Changing into her pajamas had obviously been a big mistake. It was like her brain felt the silk on her skin and was immediately programmed to pass out. But Leo still hadn't shown up, and she was on chapter five. It wasn't like him not to at least check in at night before bed if he wasn't going to be staying with her. Maybe something really was wrong.

Suddenly, in her mind's eye, she saw the Darklighter they had encountered earlier. He was standing over his kill, laughing, but this time the person at his feet wasn't a young blond girl. The person at his feet with an arrow sticking out of his chest was Leo.

Just stop it, she told herself, shifting her position and ignoring the sickening feeling in her heart. She lay on her side and propped her head on her hand, the book open flat in front of her. *Everything is going right so you just feel the need to create problems. Leo is not dead on your doorstep. He probably just couldn't get away.*

Yes. That was it. Leo was tied up in those meetings and Piper was just being neurotic. He would be here any minute now. Any second he would orb right into bed with her, wrap his arms around her, and give her a nice, big kiss. Any minute now . . .

Piper glanced up at the ceiling, wondering if Paige and Phoebe were still at it up there. Maybe if she went up to talk to them they could reassure her—tell her that they were sure Leo was just fine and she was only being paranoid. But Piper had been avoiding going back to the attic all night. She knew that eventually she was going to have to go back to being the only Piper, but she didn't have to *help* figure out a way to make that happen. Not when she was benefiting so much from having a double.

Huh. Speaking of which, Piper thought, glancing at the clock. It was getting kind of late and she hadn't heard from Piper Two in a while. The poor girl was probably still dealing with Rinaldo and his entourage and their many issues. By now they had probably demanded their own private lavatories and requested she rename the club "Rinaldo's." Piper decided to give Piper Two a call to see how she was handling it all, but also because listening to crazy Rinaldo stories would help her stay awake. Besides, maybe Piper Two could be the one to make this uneasy feeling about Leo go away. All she really needed was an affirmation of her own thoughts anyway.

Piper picked up the phone and dialed the number of her own cell. The voice mail picked up on the first ring. "Hi! You've reached Piper Halliwell. You know what to do at the beep!"

I have to change that message, Piper thought, cringing at how chipper she sounded. After the beep, she left herself a message. Just one more weirdness in a day full of weirdnesses.

"Hey, Piper, it's me, Piper," she said with a smile. "Just wanted to see how you were. No emergencies. Just . . . call me back when you get this!"

As Piper hung up the phone, she felt oddly hollow and alone.

Get over yourself, she thought. *All you've wanted for the past couple of weeks is some time to yourself, and now that you have it, you're whining.*

She sighed and pulled her book toward her again, hoping to get lost in its pages. But she hadn't read through three full sentences when once again, her eyes started to close. She yawned and strained against it, but it was no use. Even with all Piper Two's help, it had been a long day—emotionally stressful—and the exhaustion was taking hold big time.

Come on, Leo. Where are you? she thought as she slipped off to sleep. *Any minute now,* her brain repeated. *Any minute . . .*

Chapter 7

Piper and *Leo lay back in a big white bed, rubbing noses, kissing, and whispering in each other's ears. Piper felt totally at peace and at ease with the world. There was no reason to leave this bed, nothing nagging at the back of her mind. It was just her and Leo, and they were as happy as could be.*

A door opened nearby and Piper looked over to find a woman walking into the room, holding a tray of steaming hot food in front of her. The woman's face was at first shielded by her long, dark hair, but as she turned to place the food in front of Piper and Leo, Piper saw that the woman serving them was none other than herself.

Somehow, this didn't surprise Piper at all. She thanked her other self and excused her from the room. Leo lifted a silver dome to reveal piles of blueberry pancakes. He and Piper inhaled their inviting scent.

"Mmmm . . . you're such an amazing cook,"

Leo told her, planting another kiss on her lips.

The door opened again and another Piper entered, this one carrying a large trophy, which she set at the foot of the bed with a smile. Piper read the plaque on the base of the cup: Piper Halliwell. Businesswoman of the Year.

Piper's heart swelled with pride. Yet another Piper walked in. She stopped and placed a bag full of money next to the trophy—money from the Rinaldo fashion show. Then another Piper entered with a sheaf of neatly organized files—all of Piper's papers clipped and placed in alphabetical order. Yet another Piper brought a huge blue ribbon—thanks for all her help with the Star Kids event.

Piper grinned as the Pipers surrounded her. Leo beamed at his accomplished wife. All this and she hadn't had to lift a finger. Piper's life was just too good. . . .

The alarm went off and Piper awoke with a smile playing about her lips. She didn't open her eyes right away, instead choosing to revel in the happy, fuzzy warmth between sleep and wakefulness. She couldn't quite recall the dream she'd been having, but whatever it was, it had left her feeling relaxed, happy, and serene. All was right with the world.

Stretching her arms out to her sides, Piper let out a blissful groan and rolled over onto her back, but then bolted up, her heart suddenly catapulted into her throat. Her hand hadn't hit a warm body when she'd stretched. Leo wasn't in bed with her. She blinked rapidly, clearing the sleep from her eyes. From the undented pillow and the unruffled blankets on his side of the bed, he never *had* been in bed with her.

This was not right. Piper strained to think, to recall whether or not Leo had popped in during the middle of the night to check in with her, but even in her groggy state she knew he hadn't. She would have remembered if he'd woken her.

"Leo!" Piper called out at the top of her lungs, stepping out of bed. Standing in her silk pajamas, the air in her room seemed unusually cold. Piper curled her fingers into fists and shouted louder. "Leo!"

Suddenly someone appeared in the corner, but it wasn't with a swirl of white light. This person was accompanied by a puff of black smoke that could only mean one thing—he was a Darklighter. Apparently they were finally ready to stage the attack the young Whitelighter had warned them about. Too bad for him he'd appeared in the wrong sister's room. Piper took one look at the skinny, goateed, all-black-wearing evildoer and lifted her hands to blow him up.

"Uh, uh, uh!" the Darklighter said, lifting one leather-gloved hand. He waggled a finger at her like he was scolding her for her rash behavior. The condescending smirk on his face made Piper seethe. "Wouldn't do that if I were you," he said. "Not if you want to see your precious husband again."

Husband? Piper thought, the air rushing out of her.

Something inside her withered and died at that very second, but she didn't lower her hands, didn't even flinch. She wouldn't give this sorry excuse for a being the satisfaction.

I knew something was wrong with Leo. I sensed it last night, Piper thought, her stomach clenching and unclenching over and over again. *Why didn't I* do *something?*

"What the hell is that supposed to mean?" she asked, her heart pounding so hard it gave her a headache. Maybe he was just bluffing. Unfortunately the goose bumps on her skin told her otherwise.

"We have him and we're not letting him go until we get what we want," the Darklighter said, shifting his weight so that he was standing with his legs apart, arms folded over his chest. It was clear from his expression that he thought it was a menacing pose. Piper was not impressed. She had a lot more power at her disposal than this guy could ever dream of.

"Phoebe! Get in here!" Piper yelled.

She heard a door opening, followed by scurrying footsteps in the hallway. Phoebe burst in wearing a short nightie. Paige was right behind her.

"No, Paige! You stay out!" Piper shouted, causing Paige to freeze in her tracks, her face contorted with confusion.

"We're not going to let you hurt our sister," Phoebe said, her face pillow-creased from sleep. She gave the Darklighter a wide circumference as she sidestepped around him toward Piper.

"Your sister? Please," the Darklighter said. "We have bigger plans than killing your sister."

"Explain yourself," Piper demanded, her heart pounding harder with each passing moment.

"I am Shrev, a Darklighter," he said, actually nodding his head in a slight bow. "And you can let the third witch in. I know she's a Whitelighter and I swear to you I don't intend to do her any harm. Not now, anyway," he added, flashing a gold tooth.

"Yeah, like we're gonna believe that," Piper said as Phoebe stood next to her, uncertainty written all over her face.

"I can't harm her. My master wants the powers of the Charmed Ones and he can't assume her power if she's already dead," Shrev replied matter-of-factly. As if he was announcing he wanted something simple from them—like a couple of dollars or a glass of water rather than their magical powers.

"That's why that Darklighter didn't kill her yesterday," Phoebe said under her breath.

"Sharp as a tack, aren't you?" the Darklighter said.

Paige stepped into the room, one eyebrow lifted. "Figures. Somebody's always wanting our powers," she said blithely, standing next to

Phoebe. "Don't you guys just feel so loved?" she asked her sisters.

"Piper, what's going on?" Phoebe asked, her voice full of trepidation.

"This guy says he's got Leo," Piper replied, just able to get out the sentence without her voice cracking. She glared at the Darklighter, trying not to let her brain imagine the million places her husband could be, the million things they might be doing to him. "Who's this master of yours?" she demanded.

"His name is Malagon," the Darklighter said reverently, laying his hands together as if he were about to pray. "He is a demon of the highest echelon, and he has forged a prison for your husband from which he cannot orb." Shrev paused and his eyes swirled with evil. "And believe me, the man *has* tried."

Piper's heart responded with a painful thump. She couldn't handle this. The very thought of Leo all alone, trapped, trying to get to her . . . it was almost too much. But she had to stay focused, stay strong. It was her only hope of saving him.

"And if we give up our powers to this Malagon, he'll let Leo go free?" Paige asked dubiously.

"That is the arrangement, yes," Shrev replied. "You have forty-eight hours to make your decision," he said, staring Piper in the eye so intently she felt his gaze on her insides. "Your husband or your powers."

"Why forty-eight hours?" Phoebe asked.

"That is all I have to say, witch," the Darklighter snapped, spittle spraying from his mouth like venom. "I will be back for your answer in forty-eight hours. If your answer is no, your beloved Leo will die," he said, narrowing his eyes menacingly. A shiver passed right through Piper, leaving a gaping hole in its wake.

Shrev smiled as if he sensed he had finally affected her. "And I will take great pleasure in killing him," he added. And then, in a puff of smoke, he was gone.

Piper's knees instantly weakened and she reached out to Phoebe, who helped her sit down on the edge of the bed. Suddenly Piper felt like she was completely filled with tears, from her tiniest toes to the top of her head.

"I can't believe this is happening," she said, leaning forward and clutching her stomach.

"Don't worry," Phoebe said, tucking Piper's hair behind her ear and cupping her cheek. "We'll figure this out. We're going to get him back."

Piper held back the wave that was threatening to explode through her tear ducts and tried to breathe. She could feel herself starting to spiral into self-pity and she knew she couldn't go there—she wouldn't. Once she started it would be impossible to stop. And they only had two days to figure out how to save the love of her life.

"I'm gonna go get the Book," Paige said when

she saw her sister's jaw set with resolve. "I fell asleep with it in my room. The good news is, I think I might have come up with a way to fix the double Piper situa . . ."

Paige trailed off and Piper looked at her and Phoebe, realizing they were all suddenly noticing the same thing: the distinct absence of Piper Two. Piper Two should have heard her calling for her sisters and come running just as they had. Where had she even *slept* last night?

"Where is she?" Phoebe asked.

"I have no idea," Piper replied.

All three sisters tromped out of the room and down the hallway, calling Piper's name—an odd experience for Piper. She'd never met anyone with her same name before, so she'd never had any reason to shout it. There was no answer. Phoebe, Paige, and Piper searched the entire Manor, but there was no sign of Piper Two.

"What if something happened to her?" Piper asked, standing in the center of the entryway, her hand over her stomach.

"I don't know. Don't you think that if she were hurt you would have sensed it somehow?" Phoebe suggested. "You keep saying she *is* you and you *are* her. . . ."

At that moment the front door opened and Piper Two strolled in, wearing the same clothes she'd had on when she left the day before. Her hair was gathered up in a haphazard bun and sunglasses hid her eyes. She let out a huge yawn as she closed the door behind her, so far unaware of her little audience. When she turned and faced the room, she paused, hand halfway to her head.

"What's going on, guys?" Piper Two asked.

"That's what I'd like to know," Piper One replied suspiciously. "Are you just getting *home*?"

"Yeah . . . is that a problem?" Piper Two replied, puling off her sunglasses. Her eyes were puffy and bloodshot and she'd clearly not slept at all. Piper One saw Phoebe and Paige exchange a dubious look, but ignored them.

"Where the hell have I been all night?" Piper One asked, hands on hips.

"I was at that new place? Bubble?" Piper replied, dropping her bag and her leather jacket on the table next to the huge flower arrangement and almost knocking it over. "Piper, it was *intense*."

Intense? Piper One thought. *I don't talk like that.*

"Really?" Paige exclaimed excitedly. "I've been dying to check that place out."

Piper One shot her a withering glance and Paige's face fell. "I mean, for you! To let you know, you know, what the competition is doing," she added lamely.

"You were at Bubble all night? With whom?" Piper One asked.

"With Rinaldo and Douglas and these model girls who were really cool once you got to know them," Piper Two replied. She stopped babbling when she noticed three pairs of brown eyes trained on her face, all of them shocked. "What?" she said. "It's good PR. Rinaldo loves me . . . us . . . now!"

"Well, that's just great for us," Piper One said sarcastically. "But in the meantime we just found out that we had it all wrong. The Darklighters didn't want Paige, they wanted Leo, and they've got him."

"What?" Piper Two asked.

"Some demon has had some Darklighter kidnap Leo and they're threatening to kill him if we don't give up our powers, so forgive me if partying with Rinaldo isn't number one on my priority list right now," Piper One ranted.

Piper Two lost all the color from her face. "They've got Leo? Why?"

"Why don't you guys fill her in?" Piper One suggested to Phoebe and Paige as she turned for the staircase. "I'm going to go get the Book from Paige's room."

"Get my notes on the wish reversal ritual, too!" Paige shouted after her. "They're on my bedside table."

"Oh, don't worry. I'm more than ready to be myself again!" Piper called back.

She stomped up the stairs noisily, but not noisily enough to cover up the sound of her own voice from below, saying with distaste, "Wow. Am I always that cranky?"

• • •

Piper One and Phoebe hovered around the Book of Shadows, which had been returned to its rightful place on the podium in the attic. Piper Two lay back on the couch, her head propped up on her arm as she watched Paige scurry about the room, setting up the wish reversal ritual she had created in the middle of the night.

"Do we really need that many candles?" Piper Two asked her skeptically.

"The more the better," Paige replied as she placed another purple candle on the floor, completing a large circle.

Meanwhile, Piper One flipped through the pages of the Book of Shadows so fast she was barely registering what she was seeing. It didn't matter because she practically knew this section by heart. The Charmed Ones had vanquished many of the demons she was breezing by.

"Wait a minute! There it is!" Phoebe said, placing her coffee aside. She grabbed a page back from Piper One and flattened it in front of her. Sure enough, the heading read THE DARKLIGHTER MALAGON in flourishing script.

"Wait a minute. The *Darklighter* Malagon?" Piper said. "I thought that Shrev guy said he was working for a demon."

"Well, he's a demon now," Phoebe replied, running her finger down the text. "Listen to this," she told them, then began to read. "In the late nineteenth century, the Darklighter Malagon registered his one-hundredth Whitelighter kill and was exalted by the demon realm for his service to black magic. The Source rewarded Malagon by ascending him to demon status but soon regretted this move when Malagon made a play for The Source's throne."

"The Source needs a more thorough procedure for background checks," Paige quipped.

"Yeah. That kind can turn on its master," Piper Two added.

Piper One flicked an admonishing glance in her twin's direction. She still hadn't forgiven her for the very un-Piper-like behavior of staying out all night. It was just a bit disconcerting. And other than her initial surprise, she also wasn't exhibiting enough distress over the Leo situation—not that Piper One didn't have that covered big time. Piper One wasn't sure what was going on with her, but Piper Two certainly wasn't acting very Piper-esque any more.

"Malagon was banished to a middling realm for his crimes against The Source," Phoebe continued. "For the last century his Darklighter brethren have attempted to break him free of his purgatory, but have yet to find the key."

Piper One looked at her sisters. "I guess he thinks our powers are the key."

"Why not?" Phoebe asked with a shrug. "Our powers do pretty much kick butt."

"Okay, you guys! The ritual's ready!" Paige said, stepping back proudly.

The trunk that held their Wicca supplies was

covered with a black velvet blanket. In the center was the chrome pot the Charmed Ones used whenever burning was needed for a spell. In the pot was a concentrated mixture of the wish charm ingredients. The candles that surrounded the trunk were now lit, dancing merrily against the gloomy mood that pervaded the room.

"Are you sure this is gonna work?" Piper Two asked, pushing herself slowly up from the couch.

"If it doesn't, I don't know what else will," Paige said. "Come on, before these things start dripping wax all over the floor."

Piper One and Piper Two moved toward Paige and stepped over the candles. They sat on either side of the trunk, eyeing each other as if they were both on their guard. Paige and Phoebe stepped in and sat across from each other, forming a square.

"Okay, Pipers, you hold hands around the pot," Paige instructed.

The two Pipers did so. Piper One was freaked by the sensation of holding her own hands, but she told herself it would all be over soon. Things would be back to normal and she could go about the business of saving her husband.

"Now remember, you have to put your whole hearts into this or it may not work," Phoebe told them.

"Fine," Piper Two said.

"No problem," Piper One put in.

"Okay, here goes," Paige said. She lit a match and tossed it into the pot. Immediately the ingredients caught fire, sending a pungent odor into the air. Then Paige put her hands on top of one set of Piper's clasped hands, while Phoebe put her hands on top of the other set.

Piper One closed her eyes and concentrated. She concentrated on her heart. She concentrated on wishing as hard as she possibly could. She'd had enough of this messing around with her double. It might have been nice at first, but they needed to focus on Leo now. Saving him was far more important than having the time to run her stupid errands.

Please let this work, she thought. *Please let this work.*

"By the Power of Three we wish this wish be done!" all four sisters recited.

Piper felt the heat of the fire flare up, and a whoosh of wind whipped her hair back. Her heart leaped. It had worked!

She opened her eyes. The fire had been snuffed out along with all the candles. Phoebe and Paige both looked dumbstruck. Behind the smoke, Piper Two was still sitting there.

"What happened?" Piper One demanded of no one in particular.

"I don't know. It should have worked!" Paige said, standing and waving smoke from the air. "We used everything—the wish charm, the fire for potency, the Power of Three. . . ."

"Were your hearts in it?" Phoebe asked, looking from Piper One to Piper Two.

"I know *mine* was!" Piper One said.

"Well, so was mine!" Piper Two shot back.

"Maybe it doesn't work with a hangover!" Piper One said accusingly.

Piper Two scrambled to her feet. "Of course! Blame me!" she said. "You're just jealous that I was out having fun while you were stuck here baking."

"You have to be kidding!" Piper One shouted back. "You know, I'm beginning to think you *are* a warlock."

"I don't have to stand here and take this abuse!" Piper Two said. "I have things to do."

"What?" Piper One blurted, her pulse jumping forward. She stepped over the extinguished candles and followed her double. "You're not going anywhere. You have to stay and help us find Leo."

"I beg to differ," Piper Two replied, pulling the rubber band from her bun and shaking out her long hair. "There's no reason the rest of our life has to fall apart because some demon has decided to mess with us . . . *again*."

Piper One's mouth dropped open. How could she be so callous?

"Piper, this is Leo we're talking about here!" Paige said. "You know . . . risked his supernatural neck to be with you . . . has saved your life a million times . . . loves you more than anything else in the universe?"

"I know, Paige," Piper Two said. "But this is why I'm here, isn't it? So that I can live both a supernatural life and a normal one? Look, your ritual didn't work, so it looks like we're both stuck here. If I go, you guys still have the Charmed Ones to work on this, and I'll be at P3 making sure Rinaldo and his people are happy. Everyone wins!"

Before anyone could protest further, Piper Two strolled out of the attic. "Piper!" Piper One shouted. Piper Two merely raised a hand as if to dismiss her and traipsed down the stairs.

"What the hell was that?" Piper One said.

"Where's the Leo love?" Paige asked, her brow wrinkling as she looked at Piper One.

"I have to go talk to her," Piper said, unable to believe what had just occurred. Piper Two couldn't be serious. She couldn't really believe that she would be able to concentrate on anything when Leo was out there somewhere, his life in peril. Maybe the two of them had argued, but they had to work together here.

Piper started across the room, but had barely gotten three feet when she was suddenly overcome with a fierce wave of dizziness. The attic spun around her, and she could have sworn the floor was moving under her feet. She stopped and swayed, her stomach rising and falling like she was cresting the biggest hill on a roller coaster. Luckily Phoebe and Paige were there to grab her arms or she would have gone down.

"Are you okay?" Phoebe asked, clutching Piper's elbow.

Piper closed her eyes and swallowed hard, waiting for the room to right itself. Finally, mercifully, it did. The tilting floor seemed to balance itself again and everything became level.

"Yeah. I'm fine," she replied, taking a deep breath. "I just . . . I think I should maybe sit down for a second."

It's just the stress, Piper told herself, trying to quell a new spike of concern that was prodding at her brain. *You just have to try to stay calm and focus on the task at hand. And that means Leo.*

If Piper Two didn't want to help them find her husband, there was nothing Piper One could do about it. All she could do was hope that her double would come around.

I can't believe how self-righteous she . . . I . . . am, Piper Two thought as she slipped out of her clothes and stepped into the already running shower. *Last night she was all on board with using this thing to our advantage and now one little demon rears its ugly head and she's all high-and-mighty.*

As the warm water pelted her body, Piper Two tried to let the argument wash away. She had other things to concentrate on, like mentally prepping herself for a day of hard work.

What was Piper One thinking? Piper *Two* knew that if she just ditched out on her meetings with Rinaldo and Douglas today, they would take personal offense and might very well pull the show from P3. She couldn't let that happen, because if it did, she was sure Rinaldo would choose Bubble as the venue and P3 would get buried. Her club would officially be old news. Forget the Businesswoman of the Year Award. In fact, forget the business altogether. Piper was not going to let P3 go down. Not after all the blood, sweat, and tears it had taken to launch the place and keep it thriving all these years.

Piper squirted a generous amount of shampoo into her palm and lathered up her hair, closing her eyes and breathing deeply to relax herself. She massaged her fingertips into her scalp, enjoying the calming sensation.

Everything's going to be fine, she told herself. *Everything's going to be—*

Suddenly Piper was hit with a dizzy spell unlike anything she'd ever felt before. Her hands flew out and slammed into the wall and door of the shower as she attempted to steady herself. She bent forward, gasping for breath and staring down at the water droplets gathering at her feet. Soap suds trickled down her temples and into her eyes. Piper had to lower herself to the floor of the shower, pressing the heels of her hands into her eyelids to clear the painful stinging.

Breathe . . . just breathe . . . , she told herself, her brain seeming to bob on a choppy sea.

At first she thought the vertigo might just be

a reaction to her empty stomach—she hadn't eaten anything all night while she was dancing up a storm. But the spell took far too long to pass, and Piper knew it wasn't just any run-of-the-mill, low-blood-sugar dizziness. There was something wrong here. Something very, very wrong.

Chapter 8

While Phoebe rushed to get some cool water for Piper One, who kept insisting she was fine even though she couldn't seem to stand up for more than two seconds at a time, Paige went down to her room to be alone for a few minutes. There were too many emotions flying high in the attic. Too much distraction. Paige had an idea and she wanted to try it out in the peace and relative silence of her own four walls.

Closing the door quietly behind her, Paige went over to her bed, sat down Indian style in the center of her plush velvet comforter, and took a few deep breaths. She listened to the sound of the running shower and tried to let its soothing monotony calm her nerves. Laying her hands flat on her knees, she straightened her back and shook her hair off her shoulders. Soon her heartbeat stopped racing and she felt her tension begin to ebb.

Don't think about the fact that there's one Piper upstairs and one showering in the next room, Paige told herself, closing her eyes. *Don't think about the total insanity of what's going on. Just think about Leo.*

Ever since the day Paige had learned that she was a witch, a Charmed One, and a Whitelighter, her life had gone a bit haywire, to say the least. But Leo had always been there for her, listened to her concerns, and helped allay them. He had supported her through everything. She didn't want to lose him any more than Piper or Phoebe did. And as a half-Whitelighter she had a special advantage that neither of her sisters could claim. She could sense other Whitelighters.

At least, she was pretty sure she could. Unfortunately she hadn't had much experience with that particular power yet. But if there was ever a time to try to hone the sensing thing, this was it.

Breathing deeply, Paige concentrated on Leo. She envisioned him in her mind, tried to reach out to him with her soul. She tried to sense him as she had seen Leo do to others so many times with his own Whitelighter powers.

Where are you, Leo? Paige thought, pressing her lips together. *Please be somewhere that I can find you. . . .*

And then it hit her—a wave of fear and love so fierce she had to gasp for breath. The sensation was somehow undeniably Leo. She knew it was him. He was the one feeling that fear—that worry. He was worried for her, for Piper, and for Phoebe. That was where the love was coming from. Wherever Leo was imprisoned, whatever they were doing to him, he was, as always, thinking of his family before himself.

"Oh, Leo. You big softie," Paige said, opening her eyes.

The tingling sensation that had covered her skin and infused her body drifted away, leaving behind a hollow fear. Paige was petrified for her brother-in-law. She knew what she had to do. She was suddenly overcome with a thrill of excitement and a clarity of purpose that made everything in her room seem to come into sharper focus.

If she could sense Leo, that meant he hadn't been taken underground—Whitelighters couldn't sense people that were trapped in the Underworld. This was good news, but even better was the fact that if she could sense him, she could orb herself to his side and bring her sisters too. This was the break they had been waiting for. She jumped off the bed and ran back upstairs to tell Phoebe and Piper the news.

"You guys! You guys! I sensed Leo!" Paige called out as she burst into the room.

"You did? Is he okay?" Piper asked, sitting up quickly. A water-soaked rag fell from her forehead into her lap and she steadied herself, having obviously given herself a head rush.

"He seems fine," Paige answered. "Just . . . you know . . . a little scared. He's worried about us, that I could definitely sense."

"Wait a minute, if you can sense him then you can orb us to him, right?" Phoebe asked, coming out from behind the Book of Shadows.

"You bet I can," Paige replied, nearing a giddy state. She loved it when she was able to contribute to the mission at hand.

"Well let's go," Piper said. She started to stand, but then swooned slightly and sat back down—hard. One hand grasped the highly waxed wooden arm of the antique sofa.

"Slow down there, dizzy girl," Phoebe said, coming over and helping Piper lay down again. "You're clearly not ready to move yet."

"Yeah, and besides, it would be suicide to orb to him without a vanquishing spell or a potion or *something,*" Paige put in.

"Okay then," Piper said, seeming at least slightly relieved to be lying down again. She was trying to sound strong, but she looked very pale and shaky to Paige. "Whadda we got in the Book?"

Phoebe walked over and flipped a couple of pages, then shoved her hands into the back pockets of her jeans as she scanned the Book. "Okay, there is a spell *and* a vanquishing potion for Malagon," she said, rocking back and forth from foot to foot.

"Gotta love a demon that needs both," Piper said flatly.

Paige's stomach clenched. "He must be pretty powerful, huh?"

"Nothing we can't handle, I'm sure," Phoebe replied comfortingly. "Wow," she added, glancing at the Book. "That's a lot of ingredients."

Paige joined her at the podium and scanned the admittedly very intricate list. It was intimidating to say the least. Still, there was nothing unfamiliar or too exotic on it. Paige felt her confidence rise another notch.

"We have all that stuff in the kitchen," Paige said. "Shouldn't be a problem."

"Finally! Good news!" Piper called out, flinging her arms straight up in the air. It created a comical pose, what with the washcloth covering her face and her legs splayed out, one on the couch, one reaching to the floor.

Then Paige noticed some printing at the bottom of the page and she leaned past Phoebe to get a better look. What she read made her heart thump once with trepidation.

"Uh oh," she said under her breath to Phoebe. She pressed her fingertip into the thick paper. "Read the fine print."

Phoebe blinked, not having noticed the line at the foot of the page before, then blanched.

"What? What is it?" Piper asked. She slipped the washcloth off her face and looked at her sisters without actually moving her head.

Phoebe pressed her teeth together, turning her lips down in a semi-wince. "We have to let it cool for six hours before potency."

There was a tense moment of silence and Paige resisted the urge to run for the door before her sister exploded. Or exploded something else in the room.

"Six hours! What the heck kind of potion is *that*? What if this Malagon guy was beating down our door right now?" Piper ranted, pushing herself up on her elbows.

"Piper, calm down," Phoebe said walking quickly to her sister's side. "That Darklighter said we have forty-eight hours to decide, so that gives us plenty of time to make this thing and get to Leo."

"Phoebe, I can't wait six hours," Piper said, her eyes filling with tears. "I want my husband back, dammit."

"We know you do, sweetie," Paige said, joining them. She knelt on the floor next to Piper and laid her hand over Piper's. "But it looks like this is the only way."

"I hate to say it," Phoebe added, standing up straight. "But we have no other choice."

Leo stood in his impenetrable cell, staring defiantly out at the Darklighters that surrounded him. He refused to sit, even though his legs were straining from hours in the same position. There was no way he was going to give them the satisfaction of seeing him weaken.

Beyond the line of Darklighters, all of whom were dressed in various black garb, were stone walls the color of blood. The ground was made of some kind of black ash and silt that kicked up into clouds whenever the Darklighters moved. Lit torches flickered from their sconces on the walls, which seemed to stretch upward forever. If Leo looked straight up and squinted and concentrated, he could swear that somewhere miles above, he could see a small patch of blue sky.

We're not in hell, he thought, still trying to make sense of what was happening to him. *We can't be underground, so we must be in some kind of middling realm. Some kind of purgatory.*

But how had they gotten him here? How had they conjured that mystical net that had interrupted his orb? And what was this cage made out of, anyway? It was rare for Leo to encounter a room from which he could not escape. There had to be some serious magic at work here.

It took all the effort he could summon to keep from trying to orb again. It was like part of his brain refused to believe that it was impossible. After all, to Leo orbing was like breathing—it was just something he did. But somehow the black bars that held him had been enchanted to confine him and his magic. He had already been thwarted enough times to know that.

"What are you staring at, freak?" one of the Darklighters spat at Leo. He was a tall, broad specimen with long, scraggly red hair and stubble on his chin. He wore tarnished bronze plates over his chest and shoulders as if he thought he was some kind of medieval gladiator. He approached the cage menacingly, reaching for the sword that was sheathed to his back.

Leo simply gazed back at him. If these Darklighters meant to hurt him, they could have done so a hundred times over by now. He was not going to flinch. There was no way he would grant them the satisfaction.

"I *said* what are you staring at, freak?" the Darklighter shouted gruffly, getting right in Leo's face between the two nearest bars.

Again, Leo didn't answer. His captors seemed to take pleasure in taunting him. Every once in a while they would get bored and something like this would happen. He was almost getting used to it.

But there was no point in talking to these people. The only person . . . or *thing* . . . worth talking to was the demon Malagon. He had made a brief appearance earlier, parting the circle of Darklighters that surrounded Leo so that he could better view his prisoner. Malagon had introduced himself and, in true cocky-villain fashion, had revealed his entire plan to Leo, believing that it wouldn't matter what Leo knew since he would soon be dead. Leo loved it when the bad guys did that. It always came back to bite them in the butt eventually.

Still, that fact didn't keep Leo from being concerned about Piper, Phoebe, and Paige. He hoped they weren't actually thinking about coming here and giving up their powers for him. They knew he would rather die than deprive the world of the Charmed Ones and all the good they were yet to do.

Unfortunately, knowing that probably wouldn't stop the sisters from coming for him. They loved him. And love made you do stupid things. He knew that if the situation were reversed, he would come for Piper in a heartbeat.

"You will answer me, fool!" the Darklighter shouted, pulling his sword out with a *zing* and flashing its impressive blade before Leo. For a split second Leo was sure his throat was about to be cut. This guy was obviously getting impatient. All the Darklighters around the cage cheered, but then a booming voice cut their mirth short.

"Christov! Step away from the prisoner!"

Christov continued to glare at Leo, his lips twitching, but he finally lowered his sword and backed quickly away. The line of Darklighters parted and Malagon himself made his second appearance. And what an appearance it was.

Tall beyond belief and as broad as a giant, Malagon shook with every step the torches that dotted the stone walls around them. He had long, flowing blond hair that tumbled down his back, and his face was as chiseled as a Roman god's. He wore a robe of black furs over his clothing, and huge boots encrusted with centuries' worth of grime and blood—blood he'd spilled with his own hands, no doubt.

There was a serene look about him as he approached Leo's cage. Serene, but deadly.

"So, what do you think, my friend?" Malagon asked, arching one blond eyebrow. His eyes were the color of a frozen pond. "Do you think your true love will come to save you?"

The words "true love" sent a dart of pain through Leo's heart, but he steeled himself.

"Never," he replied defiantly. "The Charmed Ones would never give up their powers to save one soul. They know their destiny still awaits."

At least I hope *they know that,* he added silently.

"You have no confidence in your love," Malagon said mockingly. He frowned as if in sympathy for Leo. "How sad for you."

Leo silently fumed as Malagon turned his back on him and strode along the perimeter of the cage. He clasped his hands behind his back and kicked his feet out as he walked in what seemed like a happy little gait.

"Well, no matter," Malagon said, looking down at the floor with a slight smile on his face. "If they won't give up their powers willingly, they'll just have to be taken by force."

This declaration received a chorus of happy grunts and nods of agreement from the circle of Darklighters. The infusion of pure evil sent a shiver down Leo's back. If only he could warn the girls. If only there was some way for him to get out of this damn cage. . . .

"Thirty-six hours and counting," Malagon said, consulting a monstrous, ancient timepiece that was strapped to his thick wrist. He looked up at Leo, a harrowing glint in his eyes. "By that time our ritual will be prepared. I will send my minions to fetch the Charmed Ones, and either they will give me their powers, or we will take them. Either way, it should be great fun."

Leo glared at Malagon, wishing there was something, anything he could say or do to wipe that smirk off his huge face. But there wasn't. And Leo had to swallow his pride.

"I don't know about you," Malagon said, leaning in toward Leo's cage and baring his teeth, "but I can't wait to see what happens next."

Chapter 9

Piper Two stood at the edge of the finished catwalk at P3 on Monday morning, watching the models strut up and down in their colorful, skimpy outfits. She was still feeling a bit off after her dizzy spell in the shower, and the light show raging above wasn't helping her situation. The pink, yellow, and blue lights flashed and whirled, making the show seem more like a disco inferno than a fashion presentation. Piper sat back on one of the bar stools to steady herself and took a few deep breaths. Within seconds she felt fine again and was able to lift her head and focus on the show.

It's just a little dizziness, she told herself. *Don't be a wuss.*

Two new models took the stage and Piper admired their long pencil skirts and flowing tops. She couldn't help but be impressed by

Rinaldo's cutting-edge, fearless designs. He was all about bold color, fresh angles, and soft fabrics, and she had to admit, it worked.

He may be an odd, smelly little man, but he knows his stuff, Piper thought.

"Amazing, isn't he?" Marsha asked, coming up behind Piper and leaning in toward her ear. Marsha was also sporting one of Rinaldo's new designs—a red T-shirt with a swirling rhinestone pattern on one shoulder and an asymmetrical neckline. Unlike the models, however, Marsha somehow looked frumpy in it.

"It's a great line," Piper admitted, her eyes on the stage.

"And P3 gets to premiere it!" Marsha gushed. "You must be so *thrilled*."

"Yep. Thrilled," Piper told her with just the slightest hint of facetiousness. Everything was so big with these people—*fabulous, amazing, thrilling*. It was so over-the-top it came off as fake.

"So, listen. Rinaldo asked me to see if you would reconsider," Marsha said, walking around Piper's barstool so she could face her. Her green eyes were bright with that ever-present excitement. The girl had to be a caffeine addict. It was either that or she was on something harder. There was no other way to maintain that level of energy all the time.

"Reconsider what?" Piper asked.

"Modeling! We all think you would look just stunning up there," Marsha said, practically drooling as she looked Piper up and down.

"Modeling?" Piper asked, narrowing her eyes. This must have been something Piper One had discussed with Rinaldo.

Why didn't she mention it to me? Piper Two wondered.

"Yes! Remember our proposed compromise?" Marsha continued, bouncing on the balls of her feet. "You let us temporarily deconstruct your VIP area for added seating, and Rinaldo will work you into the lineup."

Piper felt her heart give a little thrill of excitement. She looked back up at the stage where three models were standing along the edge, posing, shifting, and posing again.

Piper Halliwell . . . supermodel, Piper thought, a smile playing at the corner of her lips. It was so superficial, so glam, so not her.

Which was exactly why she loved it.

Still, she also loved her VIP alcoves. That was where San Francisco's elite came to kick back. That was where she hung out with her family. That was where she'd had a million and one heart-to-hearts with everyone from Dan to Prue to Phoebe to Paige to Leo. She didn't want to give them up. At least not permanently.

Piper turned to Marsha, who appeared to be panting with anticipation. "What exactly do you mean by *temporarily* deconstruct . . . ?"

• • •

"Okay, Piper, you're up!" the show's coordinator, Sharon Wright, said, half-shoving Piper out onto the stage.

Heart pounding, Piper walked out to the center of the stage and paused, her legs shaking slightly. P3 looked so different from up here. Douglas and Rinaldo stood off to one side of the catwalk, and Marsha and a few of the models flanked the other side. Piper looked down at her outfit—a pink and yellow flutter-sleeved top and an impossibly short leather skirt—and wondered what she was thinking. Even with the spiked heels, she was still at least six inches shorter than the other girls. Did she look remotely like a model up here?

"Shoulders back! Head up! Confidence, Piper!" Rinaldo shouted out, making her feel even more conspicuous.

"Down the catwalk!" Sharon hissed from backstage, holding the earpiece of her head mike.

Okay, I can't do this, Piper thought. *Too much pressure. What was I thinking?*

Piper looked down at Douglas. He smirked at her, clearly amused that she was hesitating. He had obviously been waiting for her to chicken out.

Don't give him the satisfaction, a little voice in Piper's mind prodded her. *Wipe the self-satisfied smirk right off his face.*

Piper shook her hair back and squared her shoulders, then started down the catwalk, just hoping her heel didn't get caught along the way. At the edge of the runway Piper paused as she'd seen the other models do.

"Nice! Very nice!" Rinaldo called up to her. Piper could see her distorted reflection in the shiny surface of the sunglasses he was sporting. "Now give us some attitude!"

Attitude? Piper thought. *Ooooookay.*

Piper put one hand on her hip and jutted that hip out, looking vacantly across the bar. Suddenly she recalled playing dress-up with her sisters when she was a little girl. She, Phoebe, and Prue used to raid their mother's clothes, which Grams had packed away after her death, and put on fashion shows up in the attic. When it came down to it, it wasn't as if Piper had never done this before.

"Beautiful!" Rinaldo said as Piper turned and struck another pose, looking back over her shoulder.

An uncontrollable grin lit her face. This was actually pretty cool. She turned again, posing one last time while facing her "audience." Then she turned and strutted back down the catwalk, barely containing a gleeful laugh. Everyone applauded for her as she walked backstage. Piper knew it was partially to stroke her ego, but it was still kind of nice. She'd done it! She was a model.

Backstage, a group of workers was assembling the backdrop for the show—a collage of multicolored boards and metal scrap. As Piper walked by on her way to the dressing room, she heard a commotion up on the scaffolding and looked up. One of the men was struggling with an unwieldy board and as Piper watched, it slipped from his fingers and began to plummet to the ground.

"Look out!" the man called.

The few people below scattered to safety, but out of habit Piper lifted her hands and froze the scene. The board stopped about five feet from the ground and the workers were all cemented with stunned expressions on their faces. Piper looked around and realized there was nothing she could do to help the situation. She couldn't pluck the board out of the sky, and anyway, there was no one in harm's way anymore.

Oh well, she thought. *This is going to be loud.*

She was just about to unfreeze the room when suddenly, time unfroze itself. Piper's heart jumped as the board suddenly smashed to the ground and everyone continued moving. Piper looked down at her fingers. She knew she hadn't done that, so why had time started up again? Nothing like that had happened since Piper had first gotten her powers—back when they were still new and relatively weak.

A couple of men picked up the board and handed it up to the guy who had dropped it, and

Piper started moving again. There was nothing she could do about her powers right now and if she kept standing there, staring at her hands, someone was going to notice.

But Piper had only taken one step when the dizziness seized her again, this time much more violently than the last. The entire floor seemed to tilt up toward her and she stumbled back a few steps, holding her head.

"Hey! You all right?" one of the workers asked, basically catching her. "Those heels can be a little tricky, huh?" he joked.

Then he got a good look at her pale face, which was suddenly breaking out with beads of sweat, and he instantly grew concerned.

"Hey! Somebody get me some water over here!" he shouted, helping Piper over to a chair. It was a relief to sit down, but it didn't stop the room from spinning. Piper put her head down between her legs, squeezed her eyes shut and tried not to throw up.

What is going on with me? she thought. *What is going on?*

Piper One lay back on the couch in the parlor, clutching one of Phoebe's wish charms in her hand like a stress ball. She squeezed the little sachet and tried not to think about Leo. If she thought about Leo, he might be able to sense it, and if he sensed her worry, that would just contribute to his distress. The last thing she wanted to do was cause her supernaturally imprisoned husband more stress.

But she was scared. She couldn't help it. The love of her life was out there somewhere being held by the only beings that could kill him. Meanwhile her double was running around town acting very strangely, like she couldn't have cared less about what was going on at home.

Maybe her heart really wasn't in the ritual, Piper thought. *Maybe she really wants things to stay as they are.* Piper One hated to admit this to herself, because she hoped that someone who was essentially *her* could never be that shallow and self-centered. Unfortunately it seemed to be the case. Why else would the ritual have failed?

And now, to top it all off, she was having dizzy spells. Piper supposed they could be attributed to stress, but they didn't feel like stress symptoms. That first one had been too strong—too all-consuming. She had a bad feeling that there was something more worrisome going on here.

Maybe I should eat something, she thought, her stomach growling the moment the idea occurred to her. Dizziness could be the result of hunger—and she hadn't eaten all day.

Feeling slightly better for having a plan, Piper pushed the wish charm into her pocket and carefully got to her feet. She was happy to find that she was perfectly steady. The floor stayed where it was, the walls neglected to spin. So far, so good.

Piper walked through the dining room, where the painters were busily applying their second coat to the walls. The extreme paint smell hit her hard and she paused for a moment, but realized she was fine. Luckily the snack cabinet where the sisters kept all the crackers and pretzels and cookies was in a section of the kitchen that was far from the fumes. Piper hurried inside, yanked open the cabinet door, and started to root around for something bland. She came up with a box of saltines.

"Hey. You got any chocolate in there?" the head painter called from the top of his ladder. "I got a sweet tooth you wouldn't believe."

Recalling the size of his belly, Piper had a feeling he had a *few* sweet teeth. She opened one of the sleeves of crackers and nibbled off the corner of the first one.

"I'm sure we have something," she answered, peering back into the dining room.

"Great," the man replied, starting down the ladder.

On his way he missed the second rung. As he tried to right himself the ladder tottered to the left. The paint pan that he had balanced up top was knocked free and started to fall, paint pouring out the side. Piper dropped the cracker box and froze the room before the paint could hit the floor.

"Damn," Piper said, surveying the scene.

The paint was going to hit the tarp that covered the floor, so the damage wouldn't be too bad, but it would still be a mess. Thinking fast, Piper grabbed an industrial-sized rubber garbage can the painters had brought in and moved it a few inches so that it was in the direct trajectory of the paint pan. Satisfied, Piper went to get back to the spot where she'd been standing before the freeze, but she was only halfway there when the room suddenly started bustling again.

What the—?

Piper jumped back into position. Luckily none of the men noticed she'd moved because they were too busy focusing on the spilled paint. Piper's pulse raced as she placed her shaky hands on the countertop in front of her.

Please no, she thought. *Not now*. She couldn't deal with her powers going wonky on top of everything else.

"Good thing that garbage can was there, huh?" the painter said, shuffling behind Piper to get to the snack cabinet.

"Yeah," Piper said. She grabbed up the cracker box and headed out of the room. The last thing she wanted right now was to be surrounded by people she didn't know. She had to get upstairs and tell Phoebe and Paige what had happened.

As she headed for the stairs, Phoebe and Paige were jogging down them, having copied the spell and the potion ingredients from the Book of Shadows. Paige had decided it was the way to go since she couldn't exactly bring the Book downstairs and risk questions from the painters. Piper was just opening her mouth to tell them about her freeze malfunction when she was suddenly hit with another dizzy spell.

"Oh, God," she said, throwing her hands out and unintentionally flinging saltines across the room.

Phoebe and Paige grabbed her arms and helped her back over to the couch as Piper fought to gain control of her equilibrium. She laid her face against the cool couch cushions, trying her best not to panic.

"Are you okay?" Phoebe asked, touching Piper's burning forehead.

"I'll be fine . . . I think," Piper replied, clutching the side of the couch. She just wished the room would stop rotating like that.

"I think she has a fever," Phoebe said to Paige.

Piper's heart skipped a beat. It was never a good sign when people started talking about you as if you weren't in the room. She pressed her hands into the couch and forced herself to sit up.

"I'm fine," she said, her stomach lurching as the room tilted and swayed. "Just . . . maybe I'm getting a cold or something."

Suddenly a demon with a human female

form and red eyes shimmered into the room right behind Paige, who was hovering near the door. For a second Piper thought she was hallucinating, but then Phoebe spotted it too.

"Paige! Look out!" Phoebe shouted.

Used to this kind of warning, Paige instantly orbed from her spot to the other side of the room, just missing being swiped by the demon's athame. The thing growled in a very *un*-human way and advanced on Piper and Phoebe.

"Uh . . . Piper!" Phoebe called out.

Piper raised her hands and tried to blow the demon up. There was a slight *pop* and a wound appeared on the demon's arm, but it only threw her for a moment and she continued to advance.

"What happened?" Phoebe asked, jumping up.

"I don't know!" Piper semi-whined. She tried again and again, only wounding the thing. Phoebe landed a roundhouse kick right in the demon's gut, but it rebounded quickly and cut Phoebe's arm with its blade.

"Ow!" Phoebe shouted, slapping her hand over the wound. "That hurt!" She slammed another kick into the demon woman's chest, shoving her back into the wall.

"A wound for a wound," the thing sneered in a high-pitched voice. It lunged at Phoebe, who levitated into the air, and then Paige threw out her hand and shouted "Athame!"

The knife orbed out of the demon's hand and into Paige's. She tossed the gleaming athame to

Phoebe, who reached back and plunged it into the demon's chest. It shrieked and clutched the handle of the blade before disappearing in an explosion of purple light.

"What the hell was that?" one of the painters asked, running into the room.

"What the hell was what . . . exactly?" Phoebe said, backing away from him.

Piper, still bewildered by her lack of firepower, watched him carefully. He didn't appear to have seen anything or he'd have probably been fairly wild-eyed by now. As it was he just looked slightly disturbed.

"We heard shrieking and . . . and crashing," he said. "Are you girls all right?"

"Yeah, we're fine," Paige said with a shrug. "Just . . . horsing around."

"You know how sisters are," Phoebe put in with a sweet smile.

The painter eyed them all as if he were starting to wonder why he'd taken this job. "I got brothers," he said.

"Oh . . . well then, you don't know," Phoebe replied. She walked over to him and patted him on his broad back, turning him so that he was facing the dining room again. "Thanks for your concern," she said, giving him a little shove in the right direction.

"What is going on with your powers?" Phoebe asked, wheeling around on Piper the second the painter was safely out of earshot.

"That was a pretty weak demon. You should have been able to take her."

"I know!" Piper said, lifting her hands and letting them drop again. "I can't freeze, either. Or I can, but it unfreezes quickly, just like when I first got my powers."

Phoebe exchanged a disturbed glance with Paige, and Piper was about to tell them not to do that when suddenly her vision went blurry.

Not again, she thought, bracing herself for another dizzy spell. But this time, none came. Instead, her mind swooned, her limbs went limp, and she blacked out.

"Okay, now I'm starting to freak out," Paige told Phoebe as they hovered over Piper.

Paige's heart was fluttering nervously, causing a weird tightness in her chest. This was not good. She was far too young to be having a heart attack.

"She's okay. She just fainted," Phoebe said, checking Piper's pulse. She held Piper's shoulders and turned her on the couch, laying her head back on one of the throw pillows. Then she lifted her feet up and took off her shoes, trying to set her up in a comfortable position.

"What if she's really sick?" Paige asked, reaching over to feel her eldest sister's forehead for herself. Sure enough, her skin was hot enough to sear Paige's palm. "Maybe we should take her temperature."

"I don't know. I don't think this is something that can be treated with Tylenol," Phoebe said, standing up.

"You're thinking it's more super than natural?" Paige asked. She had the same fear, but she was hoping Phoebe wouldn't agree. As scary as a regular spiking fever was, it was even scarier if it wasn't a *normal* spiking fever. A normal fever could be dealt with at a hospital with expert help. The other kind, well, who knew how to deal with it?

"I don't know," Phoebe said, shoving her hands into the back pockets of her jeans. "It seems a little coincidental, don't you think? She makes a wish to double herself one day, and the next she's feverish and dizzy and her powers aren't working?"

"It has personal gain written all over it," Paige put in.

"I hate to say it, but yeah, you're probably right," Phoebe replied.

They both looked down at Piper, who was breathing slowly in and out as if in a deep sleep. Her skin was so white it almost looked translucent. Paige had the sudden sensation that she was staring at her sister's corpse in a coffin, and a chill ran over her skin. She had to look away. She had to *move* away. There had to be something she could do.

But what?

I wish Leo were here, Paige thought. He'd know

what to do. *Right. Leo. The other major issue of the moment.*

"I'm gonna go get the ingredients for the potion and get to work," Paige said, noticing that the recipe was now crumpled in her sweaty palm. At least she had a clear plan on the Leo situation. Working on the Malagon vanquishing potion was something productive she could do.

"What about the painters?" Phoebe asked.

"I'll just tell them I'm making pasta sauce," Paige said, looking down at the list. "A very gross, very pungent pasta sauce."

"All right," Phoebe said. "I'm going to go through the Book of Shadows one more time and see if I can't find anything that will help us figure out what's going on with Piper."

"Phoebe, we went through it twice last night," Paige said carefully. "There's nothing about a doubling potion. That wish reversal ritual was our best shot."

"I know, Paige, but there has to be something we missed," Phoebe said, her voice firm. "I can't just sit back and watch Piper suffer like this."

"I know," Paige said, her heart turning. She walked over and wrapped her arms around Phoebe, and Phoebe hugged her back tightly. "We're going to figure this out," Paige told her. "We always do."

"Okay, then," Phoebe said, pulling away and putting on her confident face. "Let's get to work."

Chapter 10

Back in her own clothes—comfy brown suede pants and a white tank top—Piper Two sat at the bar, her head in her hand, staring down at the list of things that still needed to be done before the fashion show on Saturday. Her hair was pulled back in a low ponytail to keep it from sticking to her somewhat sweaty face. Breathing evenly, she tried to stave off another wave of vertigo and read over her list.

She had to call her water distributor and make sure the extra shipment of mini Evian bottles was on its way. Calls had to be put in to the last few VIPs who had yet to RSVP to the event. She had to interview and hire extra bouncers and make up a final guest list. Piper read it all, but barely paid attention. It was hard to focus, what with the waves of heat that kept rushing over her—and the pounding headache.

Piper took a deep breath and sipped at her water. She glanced at her cell phone on the bar next to her paperwork and briefly considered calling home to see how the other Piper was doing, but decided against it. Part of her didn't want to know—if Piper One was having the same fits she was, then it was definitely something serious and she wanted to avoid dealing with it at all costs. Part of her also didn't want to get sucked back into all the drama at the Manor. There was enough drama for her right here.

"I want to lead off with the evening wear! The *evening wear*!" Rinaldo practically screamed as he and Sharon stormed out onto the stage from the wings. "Why do you keep *insisting* on contradicting me?"

"Rinaldo, you have to save your best stuff for last," Sharon told him, trying to be diplomatic. "The evening-wear line makes a stronger finish than your sportswear."

Rinaldo's face went from red to purple. Marsha rushed up to the stage with a bottle of water, clearly hoping to defray a temper tantrum.

"Here, Rinaldo, drink this," she said, holding out the open bottle tremulously.

"I will not!" Rinaldo shouted, whacking the water out of her hand and dousing both her and Sharon with it. The bottle bounced across the stage, gushing everywhere. Marsha blinked rapidly as her mascara started to streak down her face, leaving black rivers on her cheeks. "And I will not stand here while you insult my sportswear line," he spat in Sharon's face.

"Rinaldo, you know that's not what I meant," Sharon said, somehow remaining perfectly calm even though her white blouse was dotted with water. "I just think it's a more natural flow to start with the sportswear and move to the evening wear."

"Well, everyone does that and I'm not going to be predictable!" Rinaldo yelled, waving his hands in the air like a crazy person. He turned and jumped down from the stage, grabbing up his long coat and his bag. "I'm going to go get some real coffee. You people call me when you've decided to start treating me like the designer of this show."

He stormed out, heaving up the stairs, and Piper heard the outside door slam—twice. Sharon rolled her eyes and got back to work and Marsha scurried after her, apologizing for Rinaldo and wiping at her cheeks with a tissue. Piper took a deep breath and let it out slowly.

Mental note: Never work with fashion people again—especially not when there's supernatural mayhem afoot.

"That was interesting, no?" Douglas said, appearing out of nowhere and taking the barstool next to Piper's.

"To say the least," Piper replied. She was happy for an excuse to push her paperwork aside. Somehow it was only contributing to her headache. "How do you work with him?"

"Well, it's just like working with kids," Douglas said, his eyes sparkling as he plucked a swizzle stick out of an open box on the bar and put it in his mouth. "And I'm great with kids."

"Really?" Piper asked, shocked.

"No. Not at all," Douglas replied with a laugh.

Piper cracked up, surprised by the fact that Douglas could make her laugh. Then she realized that her headache had subsided and that she was feeling clear again. She took a sip of her ice water and sighed. It was amazing, the euphoria that stemmed from feeling better. Suddenly Piper felt as if she could do anything.

"So, listen," Douglas said, checking his glitzy watch as he twirled the swizzle stick between his teeth with his other hand. "I don't know about you, but I am famished. Would you like to join me for lunch?"

"Oh, I don't know," Piper said, looking down at her list of fashion show tasks.

Douglas stood and yanked down on the sleeves of his dress shirt, straightening all creases. "Suit yourself. But Rinaldo is going to be back in a few minutes. Are you sure you want to be here for that?"

"Good point," Piper said, practically jumping off her stool. She picked up her purse and leather jacket, and Douglas smiled as he led her to the stairs. Piper could do her work later. She might as well take advantage of the fact that she was feeling fine, anyway. Who knew—the next dizzy spell might lay her out for good.

But as Piper slipped into the passenger seat of Douglas's sexy little car and tipped her face toward the sun, she pushed her cares aside. Douglas flipped the stereo on and peeled out into traffic. The wind instantly lifted Piper's hair off her neck and she continued to feel better and better. Forget about Darklighters and demons and personal gain. It was great to be young and free in the city.

Phoebe dialed Piper's cell phone number for the hundredth time and held her breath as she pressed the phone to her ear. The line didn't even ring before Piper's voice mail picked up. Phoebe groaned loudly and punched the "off" button, just narrowly resisting the urge to launch the receiver across the kitchen. How could Piper Two have turned her phone off when there were so many emergencies at home? At this point there was so much going wrong, Phoebe couldn't even keep track of it all.

"I don't know why you keep calling her," Piper One said from her chair at the kitchen table. "We have the Power of Three. We don't need her to do what we have to do."

"Am I sensing a little bitterness in your tone?" Paige asked as she poured the cooled vanquishing potion into three small bottles. The mixture, which had started out a dark green color in the pot, had somehow cooled to a thick, inklike black. Paige wrinkled her nose as she corked the bottles. It was also quite pungent.

"No. I'm not bitter," Piper said, picking up a stack of paint chips the painter had left behind and tapping them against the surface of the table. "If she doesn't care about Leo, that's fine. I care enough for the both of us."

Phoebe blinked, wondering how and if that sentence even technically worked—weren't the both of them really just the one Piper?—but decided not to dwell on it. All she knew was that if Piper Two was really a Piper at all, she would have been here and she would have been just as concerned about Leo as Piper One was. Phoebe was starting to wonder if they *were* really both her sister.

"I don't know. I would just feel better if all of us were here," Phoebe said, sitting down across from Piper One. She took the paint chips, which were tapping faster and faster, from her sister's hands. Piper pulled her fingers back and laced them together. "But I guess you're right," Phoebe continued. "We do technically still have the Power of Three."

"We're all set," Paige said. She walked over and handed each of her sisters a vial of potion, then tossed hers into the air and caught it. She waggled it in front of them, arching her eyebrows. "Anyone ready for a little vanquishing fun?"

Phoebe looked across the table at Piper. She'd only woken up from her faint-induced sleep about an hour ago and she still looked pale and pasty. Her hair stuck to her forehead in places, and her cheeks were virtually devoid of color. She looked as if she had mono, or at the very least a bad case of the flu.

"What?" Piper asked, noticing Phoebe's expression.

Phoebe cleared her throat and squirmed. There was something about this situation that she didn't like. The last thing she wanted to do was send her sister into battle if she wasn't ready.

"How're you feeling?" she asked Piper as her older sister took a deep breath.

"I'm fine," she said tersely, pushing herself up. "Let's just go get my husband back. Then I will be *much* better."

She grasped her vial so hard her knuckles turned white, and she placed her other hand on Paige's shoulder. Phoebe could tell Piper was very weak and just trying to put on a brave front, but she didn't want to pound this issue into the ground. If Piper said she was ready, she was ready. Besides, it wasn't like they had much choice. Malagon's deadline for giving up their powers was rapidly approaching, and if they didn't get Leo out of there soon, they were all in trouble.

"Ready, girls?" Paige asked.

"Ready," Piper and Phoebe said in unison as Phoebe linked her arm around Paige's.

As they orbed out, Phoebe could only hope that they actually were.

When Paige's feet hit solid ground again, she found herself in a huge cave with jagged red walls and some kind of silty black substance for a floor.

Why do they always live in caves? Paige thought.

Then she noticed the army of Darklighters that stood around her and her sisters, forming a seriously menacing circle. For a split second the appearance of the Charmed Ones was such a surprise that none of them moved, but soon they had all drawn their weapons and aimed them at Paige and her sisters. It was an impressive array. Everything from crossbows to swords to maces. Paige took an instinctive step behind Phoebe. Every last one of those weapons was soaked in a special poison designed specifically to kill her—a Whitelighter.

"Leo!" Piper said, turning around.

"What are you doing here?" Leo asked. He sounded somewhere between relieved and livid.

That was when Paige saw the cage. Leo was standing inside an egg-shaped cell made out of fuzzy-looking black bars—clearly some kind of magically enchanted substance. He looked tired and haggard and had a healthy layer of peach fuzz on his chin. Paige had never seen Leo look so hobo-worthy. Her heart instantly went out to him.

Suddenly the line of Darklighters parted and a man who had to be a certified giant stepped through the opening. His long blond hair, piercing eyes, and haughty demeanor immediately brought to mind images of medieval knights that Paige had seen in books and movies. The Knights of the Round Table. Guinevere and Lancelot.

This must be Malagon, Paige thought, noticing the reverent manner in which the other Darklighters regarded him. Some even bowed their heads as he passed. The walls seemed to tremble with every step the larger-than-life demon took.

"You're early!" Malagon said cheerily, his voice booming and echoing off the walls. When he smiled it somehow made his face appear even more sinister. There was a jackal-like quality about him. "I love women who can make decisions. They're so rare," he added, stopping in front of them and folding his hands over his fur robes. "Are you ready to give up your powers, then?"

All three sisters turned to face Malagon down, and Paige, as always, felt the power of just being at their sides. This giant ex-Darklighter demon was nothing compared to the Power of Three.

He was never even going to see what they had coming.

"Piper, just go!" Leo cried out desperately. "Phoebe, Paige, listen to me! You can't give up your powers for me! They'll just kill us anyway. Don't do this!"

"We're not," Piper told him, tossing her hair over her shoulder.

Together, all three sisters reached back and flung their potions at Malagon's feet where they shattered, enveloping him in an explosion of fire. The Darklighters had started to advance on the sisters, but the blast from the potion sent them flying back toward the walls—a nifty little bonus.

Malagon let out a growling scream and struggled against the fire but couldn't break free. Still, it wasn't enough to vanquish him outright. They needed the spell for that.

Paige reached out her hands to her sisters and felt Phoebe's skin, cool and dry, and Piper's skin, hot and sweaty, touch her own. She pushed aside her growing concern for Piper and focused all her energy on the spell. Soon they would be out of here, and Leo would help them take care of Piper—and Piper.

Blood to blood, ash to ash
Evil spawned from darkness past
By the Power of Three we banish thee
Leave this realm, be gone at last!

Nothing happened. Paige looked at her sisters, whose concerned expressions mirrored her own. Malagon, his fists clenched, managed to reach up his arms and break through the wall of fire.

"Try again!" Phoebe called out, even as the magical fire surrounding the demon started to weaken and fade.

Blood to blood, ash to ash
Evil spawned from darkness past
By the Power of Three we banish thee
Leave this realm, be gone at last!

As they finished the second reciting, Malagon started to smile. The fire was almost gone now and the Darklighters were rousing themselves and advancing once again on the Charmed Ones. They did not look happy.

"You guys?" Paige said, her heart in her throat. Piper's hand gripped hers more tightly. Phoebe let go.

"Duck!" Phoebe shouted.

Malagon reached back and hurled a huge energy ball in their direction. Paige hit the ground, dragging Piper with her, and Piper just barely got out of the way, collapsing to the floor. The ball of blue energy exploded against Leo's cage, throwing him back into the bars. Leo held his arm and shouted in pain.

Paige crawled toward Piper as Malagon

stalked over to her, wielding another energy ball. Piper lifted her hands and feebly directed her power at Malagon, but it did nothing. It didn't even leave a wound as it had on the lesser demon who had attacked them earlier.

"Why isn't it working?" Piper cried weakly, clearly in the midst of an emotional breakdown. She tried again and again, each time with the same non-result.

"Phoebe! Get your butt over here!" Paige called out.

Phoebe laid out a couple of Darklighters with a few expert kicks, then ran back to her sisters. She dove to the floor to join them and wrapped one arm around them protectively. Malagon now stood directly above Piper, Paige, and Phoebe, tossing the energy ball up and down, taunting them.

"Come on, Piper. We're getting out of here," Paige whispered in Piper's ear.

"No! We can't leave Leo!" Piper cried out, tears now streaming down her face. She'd finally reached the breaking point. Paige fought to keep from losing it herself—it wasn't easy to hold on when your most levelheaded sister was in the midst of a breakdown. Phoebe looked into Paige's eyes and grasped her hand, which gave her an infusion of strength. Together, all three sisters looked up at Malagon.

"It was a nice try," he told them. "And I will forgive this little indiscretion only because I still need your powers. You now have twelve hours."

He lifted the energy ball above his head as if he was going to hurtle it down on them. Paige quickly orbed her sisters out of there, even as Piper screamed in protest.

Chapter 11

"Why did you orb us back here?" Piper cried out, throwing Phoebe and Paige off of her the second they were back in the living room at the Manor. Her face was streaked with tears and her voice had taken on a seriously unnatural pitch.

Phoebe's heart burned inside of her. She almost never saw Piper like this. Her older sister only cried in the most dire and hopeless situations. She only cried when she lost someone she loved.

"Piper, I had to," Paige said, sounding like a lost little girl. Phoebe knew Paige was just as freaked by the breakdown they were witnessing. "He was going to kill us."

"No! No! He wasn't!" Piper said, pacing behind the couch. Her arms were locked over her chest as if they were trying to hold her together. "He *said* he needed us. He *said* he still wanted our powers, Paige. How was he going to get them if we were dead?"

Piper's eyes flashed, and two pink circles appeared on Paige's milky white cheeks. "I . . . I'm sorry . . . it was just . . . he was about to throw that energy ball and—"

"And you just decided to leave Leo there?" Piper snapped.

"The spell didn't work. What else were we supposed to do?" Phoebe said, jumping into the fray.

"I don't know . . . *something*," Piper cried. "Not just leave him there! Did you see him, Phoebe? He was hurt and he was all alone and he . . ."

Finally it seemed Piper couldn't take it anymore. She covered her face with her hands and sobbed openly. Phoebe walked over and put her arms around her sister's shoulders, leading her over to the couch. Piper was still very weak and if she didn't take a rest soon, she was going to end up fainting again.

"I'm sorry, Piper. I just reacted," Paige said, leaning into the back of the couch.

"I know," Piper said through her tears. She sniffled and tried to stop the flow, taking a few deep breaths. "It's just . . . I don't understand what's going on. My powers are so weak, and we don't know how to get them back to full strength. And now the spell didn't work—"

"We don't know if that's connected," Phoebe

said, rubbing her hand lightly up and down Piper's back.

"Oh, come on, Phoebe," Piper said. She dropped her hands to her lap and turned a doubtful glance on her sister. "You think it's just a coincidence that the same day I'm dizzy and fainting and my powers are all funky, we try to do a Power of Three spell and it doesn't work?"

"Okay, maybe there is some correlation," Phoebe admitted. "But I don't want you to go thinking that this is in any way your fault."

"Yeah," Paige interjected, attempting to smile. "All we need is a plan B. We're good at plan B's."

"Exactly. All we have to do is figure out a way to get you back to full strength," Phoebe told Piper, tucking her sister's hair behind her ear. "Once we do that, we'll be all over that demon's big sorry butt."

Piper turned and leaned back on the arm of the couch, looking weaker than ever. "I appreciate what you guys are trying to do, but to be honest, I can't even imagine what it feels like to be at full strength," she said. "If anything, I feel even worse."

At that moment the front door burst open, and Paige and Phoebe jumped. They both rushed out to the entry hall and saw Piper Two being practically dragged through the door by one of the hottest men Phoebe had ever seen. But she didn't have time to dwell on the male supermodel. Piper Two had one arm hooked around his neck while the other hung limply at her side. Her head lolled over and rested on his shoulder.

"Are you her sisters?" the man asked in a British accent.

"Yes. What happened?" Phoebe asked, rushing forward.

"We were having lunch at my apartment and she suddenly just fainted off her chair," the man said, catching his breath as Phoebe helped support Piper's weight. "One minute she was talking and then she was just out. She fainted dead away."

Phoebe exchanged a disturbed glance with Paige. This was exactly what they had been afraid of. Both Pipers were experiencing the same maladies. It had "personal gain" written all over it.

"Wait a minute. Lunch at your apartment?" Paige blurted suddenly.

Yeah. What's that *about?* Phoebe thought.

"We're . . . business associates," the man said, not too convincingly. What was going on here?

"You guys, this is Douglas," Piper Two said with a smile, rousing herself slightly.

"Pleased to meet you," Douglas said flatly.

"Is she *drunk*?" Paige asked, watching the way Piper was slinging her hand across the man's chest. Completely inappropriately.

"I don't think so," Douglas said, readjusting Piper's weight on his shoulder. "Just groggy."

"Come on. Let's get her inside," Phoebe said. Enough with the third degree. They could talk about who this guy was and what Piper had been doing at his place later. Right now taking care of Piper needed to be top priority.

Phoebe and "mystery man" Douglas helped Piper Two into the living room where Piper One was already sacked out on the couch, her head against the pillows, her feet on the floor.

"Oh God. It's you," Piper One said disgustedly.

Douglas paused in the doorway. "Piper? Do you have a twin?" he asked, his brows coming together.

"Something like that," both Pipers answered in unison.

Piper Two pushed away from Phoebe and Douglas and dropped onto the couch, taking the exact same pose as the other Piper, but looking in the opposite direction. Once again they looked like mirror images of each other.

"Is she sick as well?" Douglas asked, eyeing Piper One.

"Yeah. Piiii . . . I . . . I mean Pia here has been out of it all day," Paige said, slapping Piper One on the shoulder. "Probably sympathy pains."

"It's a twin thing," Phoebe said in response to Douglas's skeptical look.

"I'm not Pia!" Piper One protested. "If anyone's Pia, *she's* Pia!" She punctuated her remark with a little kick in Piper Two's direction. Piper Two responded with a scowl.

"Well! Thanks for bringing her home!" Phoebe attempted to usher Douglas out before the situation could get any more suspect, but Piper Two bolted up in her seat.

"Wait!" she called out. Douglas turned to her, and much to Phoebe's utter shock, Piper Two grabbed his lapels and pulled him to her. She planted a long, firm kiss on Douglas's lips, then released him and slumped back down again. "I had a great time," Piper Two said.

"*What* was *that?*" Piper One shouted, sitting up. "Did you just *kiss* that toad?"

"Uh . . . I'd better be going," Douglas said, straightening up and smoothing the front of his suit.

Phoebe followed him to the door and closed it behind him, then paused and took a deep breath before returning to the mayhem in the living room. Piper and Piper were already embroiled in an argument, and poor Paige was trying desperately to mediate. It was time for someone to take control of the situation.

I guess it's gonna have to be me, Phoebe thought. *Sometimes this middle-sister thing really sucks.*

Marching back into the living room, Phoebe raised her hands in the air. "Hey, hey, hey, hey, *hey*!" she shouted, cutting all the voices short. Her eyes flashed as she looked at Piper Two.

"I think we're all wondering what the heck is going on with you," she said. Piper One arched her eyebrows, waiting for the response.

"You tell me!" Piper Two blurted. "I keep getting dizzy and my powers haven't worked all damn day."

Phoebe, Piper One, and Paige all looked at one another, a new thickness of dread settling in over the room. Both Pipers were weakening and both were getting worse. How long would it be until they both took a turn for the *worst*?

"Paige, get the Book of Shadows," Phoebe said. "We are going to figure this thing out, once and for all."

Leo sat back in his cell, cradling his broken arm and wishing he had the ability to heal himself. Having a broken bone was making it a lot harder to keep up a brave, strong face in front of the Darklighters. But even worse than the pain was the uncertainty. The uncertainty of what was going on with Piper. The thought that something might be seriously wrong.

All around him the Darklighters talked, laughing occasionally, sometimes breaking out into spontaneous wrestling matches. These guys were evil by nature—they lived for the kill—and the longer they were forced to sit around with no hopes for doing violence, the rowdier they became.

Whatever you do, just don't come back here, Leo thought, wishing he could actually *talk* to Piper and her sisters. He knew that having failed once they would try again. It was only a matter of time before they came up with a plan B. But bringing Paige back here would be suicide for her. It would be suicide for all of them.

Which they probably already knew before they ever came here the first time, Leo thought, wincing against the pain as he shifted his legs out from under him. He wasn't sure how they had found him, but he was proud of Paige, so new to her Whitelighter powers, for being able to orb them all here. Still, on some level, he wished she had failed. Then they wouldn't have been able to risk their lives for him. They would have been forced to stay back at the Manor, safe and sound. Relatively speaking.

He settled back with his head against the bars and sighed. He wasn't surprised the Charmed Ones had put themselves in danger to try to help him. After all, he would have done the same for any one of them. But he was surprised that their spell and potion hadn't worked. He knew they wouldn't have come unless they felt they were absolutely prepared. So what had gone wrong?

Piper, Leo thought.

He'd been trying to hold off the thought ever since the girls had orbed out, but he couldn't fool himself any longer. Something had been wrong with Piper. He had sensed it the moment he saw her. She was sick—frail and nearly colorless, her eyes tired and red. Was it possible that whatever she was sick with had weakened the Power of Three?

But how? She had been fine the last time he'd seen her. Could she have gotten that ill that fast?

Leo knew he could drive himself insane just thinking about it and he tried not to, but it was next to impossible. There was nothing else to do here but obsess.

Whatever you do, just don't come back here, Leo thought again, holding his breath as he moved his arm. The pain radiated up to his shoulder and into his temple. *Especially not if Piper is sick. You guys can do it without me. You don't need me to fulfill your destiny.*

It wasn't as if the thought of Piper losing him, of him losing Piper, didn't rip his heart to shreds right in the middle of his chest, but he couldn't think about that now. He couldn't be selfish. The Charmed Ones didn't need him. They would get another Whitelighter and life would go on.

Don't come back, Leo thought. *The world can't afford to lose the Power of Three.*

"There is nothing in here!" Paige said, slamming the Book of Shadows closed and narrowly missing maiming her fingers. "We've looked through it a million times!"

"This can't be right," Phoebe told her, walking over and opening the Book again. "There can't be nothing we can do. There's always something we can do."

Phoebe flipped through the pages. The flapping sounds made by the heavy pages filled the attic, and Paige took a step back. She didn't want to admit it any more than Phoebe did, but the situation looked hopeless. The book had nothing in it about a duplication spell. Without the spell they couldn't work up a reversal, and without a reversal, Piper One and Piper Two were screwed.

"Do you really think the fact that there are two Pipers is messing up the Power of Three?" Paige asked, walking across the room. She needed some breathing room, and she needed to move. The longer she stood still, the more her tension grew. At this point, premature wrinkling was definitely going to become an issue.

"What else could it be?" Phoebe asked. She wasn't even looking at the pages as she turned them. She was obviously just doing it to have something to do. "Piper was right. It's too much of a coincidence that her powers are screwy and the spell didn't work. It has to be the personal gain."

"Or some other side effect of the wish," Paige said.

She paced along the wall, mulling this over. Maybe there was still a way to reverse the wish. Could it be that she had missed something in the preparation of the ritual? Maybe if they tried it again. . . .

Paige suddenly felt a tug from behind. She tripped forward slightly, then heard a rip. She grabbed up her long white skirt and looked at the eyelet hem. There was a jagged tear about two inches long that reached from the hem straight up into the skirt. Paige looked down and saw a nail sticking out from the side of an old trunk.

"Perfect," she muttered, grimacing. The thin fabric had already started to fray.

"You okay?" Phoebe asked, looking up from the book.

"Yeah," Paige said heavily, clomping back toward Phoebe. She held up the hem. "But my skirt is trashed. It just split right up the—"

Suddenly Paige stopped, an epiphany lighting her up from the inside. Still clutching the hem of her skirt, she stood there going over the idea in her mind until she was certain she had it all right.

"Omigod, that's it," she said, spreading her fingers wide. "It makes perfect sense!"

"What makes perfect sense?" Phoebe asked, sounding tired.

"Piper! She didn't *double* herself! She split herself in two!" Paige exclaimed, her heart now pounding with excitement. "I can't believe we didn't think of this before!"

Now intrigued, Phoebe walked around the podium and stood in front of Paige, her eyes alight with hope. "Okay, what're you thinking here?"

"If Piper really had *doubled* herself, technically she wouldn't be getting weaker. She'd be at *double* power, right?"

"Right . . . ," Phoebe said.

"Look," Paige continued, holding up her skirt hem in front of Phoebe's eyes. "See? The second the skirt split, it started to fray, right? It *weakened*. Get it?"

"So you think that when Piper wished that there were two of her . . ."

"She didn't actually *double* herself," Paige said. "She was magically *split* into two people."

"That could be why Piper Two is acting so weird," Phoebe said, nodding her head as she thought it through. "Maybe one Piper got some of Piper's traits, and the other Piper got the other traits."

"Exactly!" Paige exclaimed. She hadn't even thought of that aspect. "That's why Piper One is all into being the homebody and acting all responsible and has been freaking out about Leo, while the other Piper has been off buying leather jackets and partying and running P3 and—"

"Kissing random guys," Phoebe supplied.

"It makes total sense," Paige said.

"Right. So say this theory is true," Phoebe said, walking back and forth in front of Paige. "What does it mean? Are Piper and Piper just going to keep getting weaker and weaker?"

"I don't know," Paige said. "Maybe."

"Well, that's not good. We need to reverse it," Phoebe said. "How do we reverse it?"

"We already *tried* reversing it," Paige said.

Then it hit her like a speeding train. She knew why the ritual hadn't worked. "Her heart wasn't in it," she said under her breath.

"Whose heart?" Phoebe asked.

"Piper Two's," Paige said. "It makes perfect sense. She's got all the irresponsible qualities. She just wants to keep partying. She doesn't really care about saving Leo or being part of the Power of Three."

"Omigod, you're right," Phoebe said. "We have to find a way to put them back together without the whole pure-wish loophole. Any ideas?"

Paige was at a loss. Maybe they now knew better what had happened, but it didn't get them any closer to a solution. If anything, it had gotten them further from the one they thought they had.

"Do I have to do all the thinking around here?" Paige asked.

"Oh!" Phoebe snapped her fingers and went up on her toes. "What if we rewrite the *To Find a Lost Witch* spell so that it's to reunite a witch's soul . . . or her body . . . or something?"

She bit her bottom lip as she looked at Paige. It didn't sound all that promising, but what else did they have?

"It's worth a shot," Paige said, grabbing a pad and pencil from the table. "It might be the only shot we have."

Chapter 12

As Phoebe slowly descended the stairs with Paige close behind, she tried to figure out a way to tell the Pipers about Paige's theory without totally freaking them out. For her own part, Phoebe hadn't been this scared in a good long while. If Paige's theory was correct, then it was quite possible that both Pipers would continue to grow weaker and weaker until they both . . .

Phoebe didn't want to think about it. She didn't even care if she had to live with two Pipers for the rest of her life. It was much better than the alternative.

"You okay?" Paige asked as they reached the foyer.

"Yeah," Phoebe said shakily. "I think."

Piper One and Piper Two were still sitting together on the living room couch, their postures rigid, their jaws set. Phoebe knew that look. It was the Piper-Is-Not-Happy look. Their voices were pitched low but sounded tense. Phoebe had a hunch that Piper One was reaming out Piper Two for disappearing all day and kissing other guys. The last thing these two needed was more bad news, but it wasn't as if Phoebe could keep it from them. They had to know what was going on.

"Hey guys!" Phoebe said with false brightness, entering the room as if she hadn't been hovering outside for the last couple of minutes. Paige walked in behind her and took a seat in the chair that was cattycorner from the Pipers' couch. Piper Two's face was blotchy and red with anger while Piper One still looked as pale as ever.

"What is it?" Piper One asked, her tone full of dread. All she had to do was look at Phoebe to read her like a book. There was no point in keeping up the happy-go-lucky façade.

"What's what?" asked Piper Two, who hadn't looked up since her sisters walked in.

She'd been sitting sideways on the couch to face Piper One, but now she turned and slumped down against the back cushions, folding her arms tightly over her chest. Phoebe was reminded of the stubborn pose Piper used to take as a child when she didn't get her way. She had gone through a whole selfish phase around the age of seven that had, luckily, ended quickly and never returned.

"Paige has come up with a new theory about . . . the two of you," Phoebe began, going for a comforting tone. She glanced at Paige who nodded at her encouragingly. "She thinks . . . *we* think that it's possible that you didn't double yourself."

The Pipers blinked at one another, confused. From where they were sitting, it sure looked like there were two of them.

"Then where did *she* come from?" Piper One asked, glaring across the couch at Piper Two.

"I think you may have actually split yourself in two," Paige told them.

"Ew! Paige!" Piper Two said, making a disgusted face.

"Just hear her out," Phoebe said, taking a seat on the coffee table. "It makes perfect sense."

Paige explained her theory again, just as she had to Phoebe up in the attic, using her torn skirt for reference. She candy-coated the differences she and Phoebe had noticed between the two Pipers so as not to offend anyone, but she got her point across. When Paige was done with her explanation, both Pipers were slumped back into the couch looking seriously nauseated.

"Are you guys all right?" Phoebe asked tentatively.

"Oh yeah. You basically just told us we're gonna die soon. We're fine," Piper Two said sarcastically.

"We need Leo," Piper One added flatly.

"Oh, of course! God forbid we should solve anything on our own!" Piper Two exploded. "God forbid we should be strong, independent women! Let's just go running to Leo!"

"Unfortunately, we can't!" Piper One replied, sitting up straight. "Maybe if you had been here to help us this afternoon, he'd be with us right now and we wouldn't be in this mess!"

"This again!" Piper Two cried, throwing up her hands. "You know—"

"You guys, I don't really think that arguing is the best thing for us to be doing right now," Paige said diplomatically.

No one but Phoebe heard her, however. The two Pipers were too busy arguing. Phoebe caught Paige's eye and tilted her head toward the kitchen. Paige got the message and followed Phoebe when she walked out of the room. Neither of the Pipers seemed to take any notice.

"I just don't get how you could kiss that creep!" Piper One said. "He's such a total ass—"

"Oh, so you're not upset I cheated on Leo, you're just upset about who I did it with!"

"That is so not true!"

"Okay, *what* are we going to do?" Paige whispered to Phoebe from the safe distance of the kitchen.

"I have no idea, but if we don't think of something fast, we're not gonna have to wait for them to weaken," Phoebe said. "They're going to kill each other."

"I've heard of split personalities, but this is ridiculous," Paige said with a sigh. "Don't they realize that we'd be much stronger if they would just work together here?"

Phoebe's eyes rested on the pot full of Malagon vanquishing potion in front of Paige, and something inside of her clicked. *We'd be much stronger if they would just work together. . . .*

"Wait a second," Phoebe said, her heart fluttering—a pleasant feeling after the misery and dread of the last few hours. "What if we try it again, but this time we bring both Pipers?"

"Try what again?" Paige asked, not quite hopping on Phoebe's thought train.

"Vanquishing Malagon," Phoebe said, standing up straight. "Think about it. If each Piper is half a Piper, maybe if all four of us say the spell together we'll be a complete Power of Three. Maybe then the spell will work."

"It's definitely worth a shot," Paige put in. "But shouldn't we try putting Piper back together first?"

"I'd love to, but we're gonna have to write a whole new spell and that's gonna take time," Phoebe said. "We don't have much time left to save Leo, so I think that's going to have to come first."

"But what if the Pipers keep getting weaker?" Paige asked.

The argument in the living room was still raging on. "From the sound of it, they've got enough strength for now," Phoebe said.

"Good point," Paige replied. "I guess that's what adrenaline will do for you."

She went to the cabinet and took out four clean vials, filling each of them with the thick, black liquid. She handed one to Phoebe and they headed back to the living room, full of purpose, psyched about their plan and ready to see the end of one perfectly insane day. But the second Phoebe entered the room, she stopped short. Paige almost walked right into her.

Piper One was sitting alone on the couch, silently fuming.

"Where's Piper Two?" Paige asked.

"I don't know and I *definitely* don't care," Piper said obstinately.

Phoebe glanced at Paige, her heart falling, her confidence instantly fading away. So much for that.

"Piper!" Douglas said, his eyes widening with surprise at the sight of her standing in the hallway outside his apartment. "What are you doing here?"

"If you want me to leave . . . ," Piper said, walking right past him into his spacious loft. She slipped out of her jacket and dropped it on the nearest chair, then swung her hair over one shoulder as she turned to face him. Douglas was wearing a form-fitting black sweater and a pair of jeans and looked incredibly sexy. It was the kind of thing Leo would never wear. Leo was too bland to even think of it.

"No, of course not," Douglas said with a smile. He picked up a remote control and pointed it toward the wall, lowering the volume on the sultry jazz music that was playing on the stereo. "I'm glad to see you're feeling better."

"I guess all I needed was a little rest," Piper said.

In truth she was still a bit shaky on her feet, and she wasn't entirely sure that getting behind the wheel of an automobile had been the best idea. As she'd driven across town her sight had seemed a bit blurry and she'd taken a couple of wrong turns. But she'd fought through the grogginess and gotten here safe and sound. She knew her sisters would be worried about her, but at the moment she didn't care. Hanging out in a nice, peaceful apartment with a chill, sophisticated man like Douglas was a lot better for her health than being at the high-stress Manor.

She couldn't listen to Piper One's admonishments anymore. And she couldn't handle the reproachful way in which her double was always looking at her. Didn't Piper One ever want to have any fun? Wasn't she sick of being a repressed goody-goody? If Paige's theory was correct, it was quite possible that she only had a little time left. She wasn't going to spend it sitting in that stuffy old house worrying and feeling miserable.

She'd had enough of that for one lifetime.

"Would you like a drink?" Douglas asked. He moved over to the highly polished oak bar and poured himself a scotch, then turned his back to her to chip some ice from a block in the freezer.

"Sure, thanks," Piper replied, resting her elbow on the back of the couch and twisting a strand of hair around her finger.

"Good choice," Douglas said, turning to face her. "One last drink before you die."

Piper jumped up from the couch in fear, giving herself a massive head rush. She brought her hands to her temples, trying to steady herself as she looked at Douglas. His face had contorted, springing a thousand nasty wrinkles and boils, and his eyes had gone black. He wielded the ice pick, tossing it from hand to hand as he crossed the room toward her slowly.

"What are you?" Piper asked, backing around the couch. Her heart hammered painfully against her ribcage and for a moment she was sure she was about to faint again. This whole double thing was really messing with her reflexes.

"Just an average, ordinary, run-of-the-mill warlock," Douglas replied, licking his lips. "You, however, are a Charmed One. No average, ordinary witch."

"How did you—"

"I walked in on a little freeze you did earlier today," Douglas explained, following her as she backed her way around the room, heading for the door. "A wicked little power, I must say. But until I saw your sisters and your duplicate I had no idea you were a Charmed One. I'm going to be the talk of the Underworld once I take what you have to give."

Douglas lunged at her then. Piper reached out to freeze him. It worked, but for less than a second. Piper screeched and jumped out of the way, but Douglas was on top of her in an instant. He tackled her to the ground as Piper kicked and flailed uselessly. He reached back with the ice pick. Piper screamed and grabbed his arm with both hands, pushing with all her might.

Unfortunately she didn't have a whole lot of might left in her. She was weak, exhausted, and dizzy. As the ice pick drew closer and closer to her face and Douglas's sneer of triumph grew wider and wider, Piper felt tears slipping down her cheeks. This was it. This was how she was going to die.

Why did I ever leave the house? she thought, wishing for the first time that she had listened to her doppelganger. Thoughts of Phoebe, Paige, and Leo flitted through her mind. For the first time in the last couple of days she recalled how important they all were to her. How much she loved all of them. How could all of that have taken such a backseat to everything else?

What's going to happen to Phoebe and Paige? What's going to happen to Leo? Why didn't this all come to me before *I stormed out?*

Apparently the conscience really came forward in the face of death.

"Just die!" Douglas shouted, thrusting the ice pick toward her.

Piper closed her eyes and waited for the pain that was about to come, but then, suddenly, something hit Douglas—hard—and he tumbled off of her to the side.

Douglas grunted. "What the—"

Piper opened her eyes, ready to smile, fully expecting to see Paige and Phoebe and Piper One having come to her aid. Instead there was a scraggly-looking man in a black coat hovering above her, pointing a crossbow at Douglas's chest.

"She belongs to my master," the man sneered.

A Darklighter, Piper realized. *Why is he saving me?*

Then it all came back to her in a rush—Piper One's encounter with the Darklighter that morning. They were keeping Leo as blackmail so that she and her sisters would give up their powers. He wasn't here to save her, but to kidnap her.

"I don't think so," Douglas said, struggling to his feet.

Douglas lunged at the Darklighter. Piper didn't wait to see what the result was. She jumped to her feet, fighting off the inevitable dizziness, and sprinted for the door. Her pulse pounded through her veins as sounds of a struggle followed her. Piper focused on the doorknob. It was only four feet away . . . three . . . two. . . .

"Ow!" Piper cried out, her head snapping back. Someone had grabbed a fistful of her hair and yanked her backward off her feet. Tears of pain sprang to her eyes again as she was yanked against the Darklighter's body.

"Where do you think you're going?" the Darklighter asked through his teeth. He smelled like onions and sweat and something acrid, like ash. Piper struggled but to no avail. There was no fight left in her weakened body and the Darklighter was far too strong.

"What do you want?" Piper asked defiantly.

"It's not what I want. It's what Malagon wants," he said.

Then a cloud of black smoke enveloped them, and the room, including Douglas's dead body, faded from view.

"Where would she have gone?" Phoebe asked, her panic level clearly escalating as she paced the living room. Piper watched her sister as she moved the curtains aside and looked out the window as if Piper Two were just sitting out on the sidewalk biding her time.

"Why does it matter?" Piper asked weakly. "According to you guys we're doomed anyway."

"Not necessarily," Paige said, sitting next to Piper. She clicked off her cell phone, having unsurprisingly had no luck, and tucked it into her bag. "We have a new plan to rescue Leo, but we need Piper Two to do it."

This got Piper's attention. She sat up slightly, her heart giving an extra thump. "A new plan? What is it?"

"We think if we all recite the spell together—all four of us—it might work," Paige explained, pulling the vials of potion out of her pocket. "If each of you is technically half a Piper, then the two of you working together should equal one full-power witch."

"So the four of us together are the Power of Three," Phoebe put in, turning to Piper. "But we need to find her. And fast."

Piper pushed herself up until she was sitting straight. She wished she could sense Piper Two the way Leo and Paige could sense the rest of them. *Wait a minute. . . .*

"Paige? Can't you sense her?" Piper asked, raising her eyebrows.

"I've been trying," Paige admitted woefully. "I think her signal's too faint. I haven't been able to get anything."

"Come on, Piper. Where would you have gone?" Paige asked, sitting down across from her sister and taking Piper's hand in both of hers.

Piper took a deep breath and thought through everything Piper Two had said. Whenever the girl opened her mouth she sounded to Piper like the little rebellious voice that had always been lurking at the back of her mind, but which she had always ignored—the voice that told her to ditch work, to buy things she couldn't afford, to just *live* a little more. Luckily Piper's responsible side had always been much stronger and more prominent than that voice could handle. But now it seemed like her rebellion was walking around in human form.

"Maybe she's at Douglas's," Piper suggested,

glancing at Phoebe. "She was acting all defiant. That's probably where she'd go."

"Great! Douglas. What's his last name?" Paige asked, grabbing her cell phone again and standing up.

"Brittany, I think," Piper said, her eyes narrowing as she thought back to her first encounter with him. "Yeah, it's Brittany."

As Paige started to dial, Piper felt a little spark of hope alight within her. Maybe her sisters' plan would work. An hour from now, they might all be sitting her together, laughing over the events of the past couple of days. She could practically *feel* Leo's hand in hers. . . .

"It's just ringing," Paige said, crossing her free arm over her stomach.

At that moment a Darklighter appeared right behind her and wrapped his arm around her throat, a thick blade shining in his hand.

"Paige!" Piper shouted as her sister dropped the phone. Both Piper and Phoebe jumped up, but there was no point. At that moment four other Darklighters popped into the living room, circling the Charmed Ones, their weapons drawn.

Piper's eyes met those of Shrev, the Darklighter who had first threatened Leo's life. Her spark of hope was doused with a heavy dose of dread as Shrev smiled slowly, triumphantly.

"Malagon's tired of waiting," he said. "It's time to go."

Chapter 13

Moments later Piper One found herself back in Malagon's lair, her arms pinned behind her by a big, burly Darklighter with skin the color of coal. She struggled against him to no avail. Each time she moved, he growled in her ear and held her arms more tightly until she thought the tendons in her shoulders would surely tear. Paige and Phoebe were being held next to her in the same way, each of them wincing in pain.

The Darklighters dragged their prisoners farther into the room, then lined them up so that they were facing both Leo's cage to their right and the squadron of Darklighters who had lined up to their left. Standing in perfect rows, their feet spread and their hands behind their backs, the Darklighters looked more like an army than ever. Their clothes were still ragtag, their faces smeared with dirt and grime, but they appeared ready for a fight.

Piper looked at Leo and saw the resignation reflected in his eyes. There was no way they could win.

"My guests have arrived!" Malagon's voice boomed against the walls. He walked out of an archway to the left of his troops and crossed behind them. As he walked through the aisle between his men and Leo's cage, his mouth stretched into a broad grin. "Forgive the manner in which you were brought here, but I simply couldn't wait any longer," he said, stepping up in front of the sisters and their captors. "The time has come, Charmed Ones," he said, smiling sadistically down at them. "You will relinquish your powers or you will stay with us and watch your beloved Whitelighter die."

Piper's heart turned and twisted painfully inside her chest. It took all the strength she had left in her weakening body to keep herself from crying.

"Trust me when I tell you I have plenty of willing executioners," Malagon added. He looked around at his followers as if considering upon whom he would bestow the privilege of murdering her husband. To Piper's disgust, all the Darklighters seemed to straighten up a little taller, hoping to impress their boss.

"So, I believe you have a spell that relinquishes your powers," Malagon said happily, clapping his hands together as he faced them once again. He reached up and summoned a young Darklighter who was standing near the archway where Malagon had first appeared. The Darklighter scurried over and handed Malagon a large box made out of thick wood. It had an ornate iron clasp. He opened it to reveal a black velvet lining.

"You say the spell, this box will trap your powers—and I believe it will be the perfect bargaining tool to secure my freedom from this . . . prison," he said, casting a sneer around the cave.

"Well?" he said, raising his eyebrows. "Start reciting."

"In your dreams," Paige spat.

Malagon's eyes darkened instantly and he stepped over to stand in front of Paige. "I believe you of all people would want to keep your mouth *shut*!" he spat in her face. "Unless, of course, you want to recite the spell first," he added, changing his tone to sickeningly sweet.

"And if we do . . . if we recite the spell . . . you'll let all of us and Leo go?" Piper asked.

"Piper, no!" Leo said.

"That is the deal, yes," Malagon said, walking back in her direction with the box. "Would *you* like to go first?"

Piper looked into the black velvet depths of the box, wondering what it really mattered. Piper Two wasn't here, which meant they couldn't fight Malagon and his army. And the more time that passed, the weaker she became, the more she could feel the end looming near. She was going to die. She was going to die because of a stupid wish. The least she could do was save her sisters and Leo before it happened.

Piper opened her mouth to say the spell—the one she'd memorized years ago when she was still uncertain about whether or not she wanted to be a witch. Leo yelled at her to stop. Phoebe whimpered her name. And then, something happened that caused her to snap her mouth shut.

Another Darklighter popped into the room in a puff of smoke, grasping Piper Two by a clump of hair at the back of her head. His face was all triumph.

"I've got her! I have the eldest!" he called out.

The room went silent. All the Darklighters looked from Piper Two to Piper One and back again. The Darklighter who had brought Piper Two dropped his mouth open and Malagon's face went slack.

"There are *four* of them?"

Suddenly Piper One's knees went out from under her and she started to fall. She would have hit the ground if not for the Darklighter that was clutching her arms. Piper Two, meanwhile, struggled weakly against her captor.

"Piper?" Leo called out, utterly confused.

Piper One's heart felt as if it were ripping in two at the sound of his voice.

"It's okay, Leo," Piper Two called out. "My heart's more than ready."

Piper One felt her chest fill with warmth. She

looked at her double and knew. Her feelings were reflected from across the room. Piper Two was ready to make the wish.

But how? They didn't have the—

Wish charm, Piper One thought. Suddenly the charm she'd shoved in her pocket earlier felt like it was burning a hole through her thigh.

"Paige? Little help?" Piper One said. She only hoped Paige would get the message. She needed a distraction.

Paige nodded resolutely. She orbed out and reappeared behind the Darklighter that held Piper Two. Before anyone could react, she yanked his sword from the sheath on his back and knocked him out with the butt of the handle. Piper Two fell forward, then scrambled up and ran toward Piper One.

"Stop them!" Malagon screamed. "Stop them!"

Paige orbed out again as Phoebe's captor made the mistake of letting her go in order to rush Piper Two. Phoebe took him down with a kick from behind, then levitated into the air and took out Piper One's Darklighter with a swift kick to the head.

"Thanks," Piper One said, rushing toward Piper Two with what little strength she had left.

"What's the plan?" Phoebe shouted as the Darklighters advanced on them.

"Just give me one second!" Piper One shouted back.

She met Piper Two right in front of Leo's cage

as Phoebe did her best to fight off the Darklighters.

"Ready?" Piper One asked, looking into her own eyes.

"Ready," Piper Two replied firmly. "I want to go back to the way things were. I want to care again."

Piper pulled the wish charm out of her pocket and clapped her hand to Piper Two's, the charm between their palms.

"I wish there were one of me!" they both shouted.

And then, Piper was there alone. No blast. No fanfare. It was just like when she had made the first wish. Nothing had happened. Nothing except for the fact that she felt whole again.

And mighty powerful.

The weakness and dizziness and nausea were gone, replaced by a fullness, a sizzling shot of heat that infused every cell in her body with energy.

"Piper!" Phoebe and Paige called out at the same time. They had both been seized again, but the Darklighters that had been bearing down on Piper had stopped, stunned that one of her had just disappeared.

Piper stood up, tossed her hair behind her back and smiled. She was whole again. There was only one Piper Halliwell, and she was in the mood to kick a little Darklighter ass.

"You called?" she said, looking at her sisters.

Before anyone could react, Piper had lifted her hands and blown the first five Darklighters in line to Kingdom Come. The rest of the Darklighters fumbled for their weapons. Piper turned to Paige.

"Paige, orb!" she shouted.

Paige did as she was told and disappeared from her Darklighter's arms in a swirl of light, reappearing at Piper's side. They both ducked as arrows whizzed over their heads.

"You got the potion?" Piper asked, holding out her hand. Paige smiled and slipped a vial from her pocket into Piper's hand.

"Good to have you back together, Sis," she said.

Phoebe shouted and Piper looked up to find her sister kickboxing the crap out of two of the Darklighters. She seemed to have the upper hand for the moment. Meanwhile, however, Malagon was advancing on Phoebe from behind, wielding an energy ball and looking seriously pissed off. A group of Darklighters were scrambling around Paige and Piper, weapons drawn, while a couple more were opening Leo's cage, undoubtedly to get close enough to kill him.

"All right, enough of this," Piper said. She reached her hands up and froze the room. This time her power worked and all the bad guys were suspended mid-action. Leo froze as he tried to pull his good arm away from one of the Darklighters.

"Phoebe! You have your potion?" Piper called out.

Phoebe ran over and joined her sisters, holding up the small vial.

"Okay, we're going to recite the spell and then we are going to orb right the heck out of here, got it?" Piper asked, loving the clarity and focus her mind was displaying. Paige and Phoebe both nodded, smiling at each other, happy to have Piper back in functioning form.

"Hang on while I get my husband," Piper told them.

She walked over to the now-open cage and unfroze Leo.

"Piper," he breathed, the moment he saw her. Then he pulled her to him with his good arm and wrapped her into a passionate kiss. It was all Piper could do to keep from laughing with glee. She had Leo back. Everything was going to be fine.

"What happened?" he asked, pulling away.

Piper had no idea how to explain it all to him. That Piper Two's near-death experience—her own near-death experience—had finally made her remember what really mattered. How her heart had realized that she had to come back together—to save Leo, to save her sisters, to save the Charmed Ones.

"I'll explain later," Piper told him. "Right now we've got a demon to vanquish."

Holding hands, she and Leo walked back

over to Paige and Phoebe. Together they tossed the potion at Malagon's feet. He immediately reanimated, looking down in surprise at the fire that enveloped him.

"This won't work, witches!" he shouted. "Don't you ever learn?"

"Believe it or not, we do," Piper replied.

And together she and her sisters recited the spell once more.

Blood to blood, ash to ash
Evil spawned from darkness past
By the Power of Three we banish thee
Leave this realm, be gone at last!

Malagon screamed as the fire grew more intense and rushed in on him. Right before their eyes, he was reduced to a skeleton that blackened to the point of no return, then crumbled into a pile of ash, indistinguishable from the substance that covered the floor of the cave.

"That was icky," Paige said, wrinkling her nose.

"Let's get out of here before the Darklighters unfreeze," Phoebe suggested.

"I'm all for that," Leo told them, wrapping his arm around Piper's shoulders.

Piper had never felt so safe, so right, so whole as she did in Leo's arms.

"Come on," she told him, rubbing his chest with her palm. "Let's go home."

• • •

"It was so cool," Paige shouted over the music that was pumping louder than ever at P3. "The two of you slamming your hands together like that. The determination in your eyes . . . ," she said, nodding her head.

Piper laughed, covering her mouth with her hand. It had been almost a week since their fight with the Darklighters, and Paige hadn't stopped talking about it since. She seemed to think Piper was some kind of superhero for overcoming the odds at the last moment and taking the situation in hand. Piper had to admit she did feel kind of cool whenever she thought about it. She had, in fact, saved the day.

"Well, I think this is the coolest thing *I've* ever seen," Leo said, sliding Piper's Businesswoman of the Year plaque off the bar and holding it up. "I'm so proud of you," he said, smiling down at Piper before planting a kiss on her waiting lips.

"Me too," Phoebe added, wrapping her arms around Piper as Paige looked on, smiling.

They had just come from the ceremony in the ballroom at the Four Seasons. Piper had given a quick, grateful speech after accepting the award, then posed for pictures with the editor of the paper and various winners from the past. She still couldn't believe she was considered to be in the same league with some of the amazing women she'd met that night.

"I'm proud of me too," she said, looking around the club.

P3 was absolutely packed for Rinaldo's fashion show, and the anticipation in the air was palpable. They had shut the doors half an hour ago when the place had been filled to capacity, and the bouncers had their hands full turning away disappointed customers. Piper only hoped that the mini Evian bottles lasted and that no one slipped on the shiny new floor.

"Piper Two did an amazing job setting this up," Paige said, studying the new lighting tracks that hung from the ceiling.

"Hey! *I* did a fabulous job," Piper said, lightly whacking Paige's arm. "She was me, after all. I am her."

Leo, Paige, and Phoebe all gazed at her, their faces masks of concentration as they tried to grasp the concept. Piper laughed. She still had a hard time grasping it herself, but she felt as if she had been in two places at once for two days. She remembered everything that happened at the Manor—the painters, the baking, the TV watching. But now she also remembered her lunch meeting with Gina, her dinner with Douglas, her night of raucous fun at Bubble. She could even remember her telephone conversations with herself from both ends of the conversation. Her brain hurt every time she thought about *that*.

"I don't get it," Paige said, sitting down on a stool at the bar. "The Piper I know never would have done the stuff Piper Two did."

"I don't know. It was kind of fun to let loose

for a little while," Piper said with a shrug. "I think I should do it more often."

"My sentiments exactly," Phoebe said with a nod.

"But not too much, right?" Leo asked. He was still a little tense after having heard that Piper had kissed another guy. He seemed to accept the temporary insanity plea, but it had put him on edge nevertheless.

"No. Not too much," Piper told him, standing on her tiptoes to give him a reassuring kiss. "Trust me, I know what's important."

Leo wrapped his arms around her waist and held her close, smiling his private smile. Piper knew in that moment that he definitely forgave her. She had the most understanding husband in the world. Thank goodness she'd had the sense to marry a supernatural being.

"Hello everybody, and welcome!" Susan had appeared on the stage, and the music was lowered to a less deafening level. The audience broke into wild applause, and Piper felt her pulse speed up ever so slightly.

"We'd like to thank you all for coming to the unveiling of Rinaldo's new spring line!" Another round of shouts and applause.

Well, here goes nothing, Piper thought.

"There *is* something I have to do, though," she told Leo, giving him a little squeeze. "But I promise it's not that bad."

Leo's face fell slightly. "What?" he asked. "What is it?"

"You'll see," she said, pulling away from him. She waved her fingers at her sisters, both of whom stared back at her blankly as she turned and traipsed through the crowd.

Piper rushed backstage, her heart pounding. She tripped on her way into the dressing room, nearly taking out an entire rack of clothing that was neatly organized into sections labeled with each model's name.

"Where have you *been*?" Rinaldo shrieked the second he saw her. "She needs makeup! Hair!" he shouted at the people milling around the lighted mirrors that lined the walls. "Get her dressed, people! Come on! What am I paying you for?"

Within seconds Piper was out of her responsible Businesswoman of the Year dress and was sitting in a chair wearing nothing but a thin white robe. Two makeup girls attacked her face from both sides with huge brushes and wedge-shaped sponges, while a tall man with a goatee yanked at her hair.

What am I doing? Piper asked herself as she watched her face slowly transform. Her cheekbones became more prominent, her eyes widened slightly, and her lips grew pouty and moist. By the time the makeup artists were done she did, in fact, look like a supermodel.

Piper couldn't help smiling at her reflection. *Oh yeah.* That's *what I'm doing*. She was playing dress-up. And she was taking a chance. If there was one thing she had learned earlier this week, it was that taking chances could be fun *and* empowering. Within reason, of course.

Marsha helped Piper into her outfit and held her high heels while she stepped into them.

"You're up next," Susan told her, rushing into the room. "Let's get you out there."

Piper had never felt her pulse fluttering away like this—not even with all the demons she had faced over the years. Warlock boyfriends and blinking fiends were nothing compared to an audience of catty fashion people. Piper tiptoed through the wings and peeked out at the crowd.

"Okay, I can't do this," she said, swallowing hard.

"Piper! You're gorgeous!" Rinaldo trilled, walking over to her with his arms outstretched. Piper held her breath as he double air-kissed her. He held her by the shoulders and looked her in the eye. "Now get out there before there's a hole in the program and I am forced to withhold your half of the profits."

"Okay then!" Piper said brightly.

Susan picked up her backstage microphone and winked at Piper. "Ladies and gentlemen, please welcome the hostess of tonight's event, the owner and manager of P3, Piper Halliwell!"

Somehow Piper forced herself to walk out onto the stage. Her knees were quivering and she was sure she was going to trip herself, but she made it to the center of the platform. The lights blinded her and she tried not to squint as she sauntered down the catwalk. The audience went wild for her, applauding and shouting as she strode by. The farther she went without falling, the easier the performance became. She could do this. She *was* doing this.

Piper Halliwell, supermodel.

At the end of the catwalk, Piper struck a pose and looked out at her family who were still standing by the bar, hooting and howling. Phoebe was clapping her hands above her head and Paige was screaming at the top of her lungs. She caught Leo's eye and he looked back at her with unabashed admiration.

"I love you," he mouthed.

Piper's heart warmed and she felt inflated with happiness and pride. She winked saucily at Leo, turned and struck another pose, then blew him a kiss. The crowd went wild all over again and Piper strode back down the catwalk.

It was over. She'd done it. She'd managed to pull off the fashion show, the Businesswoman of the Year Award, and the Star Kids event. She'd saved her husband, vanquished a powerful demon, and destroyed a few Darklighters as well. And now, she was even conquering the fashion world. Kind of.

Piper stopped before exiting the stage, turned, and waved to the crowd with a huge, triumphant grin. It was good to be Piper Halliwell.

THE BREWING STORM

Despite wacky weather threatening the San Francisco area, life for the Charmed Ones is as normal as ever. Normal, that is, until eleven-year-old Tyler Michaels shows up at their door. Tyler, a Firestarter, is on the run from demons. Though the Halliwell sisters have dealt with Tyler before, a glance at the Book of Shadows turns up new, unexpected information about the boy . . . and the forces for which his magic can be harnessed.

Once a century the planets align in such a way that the tides shift and the climate changes, causing unpredictable weather and earthquakes. With the world out of balance the Fire-starter is charged with gathering the other Elementals on the Night of the Aeolus to perform a sacred ritual. Without this ritual the weather will eventually tear the world apart. But the demons chasing Tyler want to divert the Elemental power and channel it for a dark evil. The Charmed Ones must prevent this from happening at all costs–but the Night of Aeolus is already upon them . . .